The Misadventures
of the
Magician's Dog

The Misadventures of the
Magician's Dog

FRANCES SACKETT

Holiday House / New York

Library of Congress Cataloging-in-Publication Data

Sackett, Frances (Frances Elisabeth), 1970–
The misadventures of the magician's dog / by Frances Sackett. — 1st ed.
p. cm.
Summary: On his twelfth birthday, Peter chooses, or is chosen by, a strange, talking
dog that teaches him magic in order that they might rescue a self-destructive wizard,
aided by Peter's younger sisters, Celia and Izzy.
ISBN 978-0-8234-2869-4 (hardcover)
[1. Magic—Fiction.   2. Dogs—Fiction.   3. Brothers and sisters—Fiction.
4. Adventure and adventurers—Fiction.   5. Families of military
personnel—Fiction.]   I. Title.
PZ7.S1193Mi 2013
[Fic]—dc23
2012041540

To Alice and Sebastian,
who inspire and delight me.

And to my mother and father,
with gratitude and love.

ACKNOWLEDGMENTS

If I were to properly thank all the people who've helped me as a writer over the years, my acknowledgements would be longer than this book. That said, Sylvie Frank, you were the real magician here: your insightful edits, comments, and questions made *The Misadventures of the Magician's Dog* into the novel I always wanted it be. Thank you, truly! Thank you too to Julie Amper (my book's lovely stepmother), Mary Cash, and all the wonderful people at Holiday House who believed in this novel until, like the Velveteen Rabbit, it finally became real. As for Sara Crowe: you're the most amazing agent in the universe, and I'm profoundly grateful for your determination to find *The Misadventures of the Magician's Dog* the right home.

Steve Valdez, thank you for the handholding, the foot rubbing, the laughter, and the love. You make me believe that anything is possible. Sebastian Hawn, reading this novel to you was one of the most magical moments in my life: thank you for the brilliant, perfect questions you asked as you listened. Alice Hawn, thank you for always sharing your big, beautiful imagination with me and for bringing so much joy into my life. Mom and Dad, thank you for everything you've done for me—including reading multiple drafts of this novel!—but thank you especially for raising me in a house full of books. Cass Sackett, Molly Sackett, Andy Pasquale, River Pasquale, Sage Pasquale, Evie Sackett, Henry Sackett, and Miles Valdez: I love you all and will be forever grateful for your enthusiasm and encouragement. I also want to thank the extended and wonderful Sackett clan for their support, and especially my grandmother, Barbara Sackett, who isn't here to see this book get published but who meant the world to me.

Matthea Harvey, I hope you know how deeply grateful I am for your endless faith in me. Julie Shigekuni, you've taught me so much as a writer and a person—and this book wouldn't exist without your daughters. Leonard Chang, thank you for your friendship and insight, and also for making me finish. Deana Sackett, I truly appreciated the time you spent catching so many of my mistakes! Brooke Wirtschafter, thank you for taking walks with me and for being the world's foremost expert on preadolescent boys. Xena Carter, thank you for encouraging me to follow my heart. Graeme Stone, thank you for always making me laugh. I also want to thank Lori Snyder, Dan Horch, Bruce Brodie, Hilary Hattenbach, Josh Hauke, Cindy Lin, Elizabeth Ross, Jason White, Lilliam Rivera, Mary Shannon, Linda Davis, Amy Spiegel, Neal Peyton, David St. Pierre, Anouk Flood, Kirstin Bucci, Rob Casper, Lindsay Cooper, Bob Johnson, Dan Gil, Kimmi Stewart, Karsten Bondy, Jonathan Wilks, Katherine Frame, Jeanne Kuntz, Rita Crayon, Edith Cohn, Michael Storms, Leo Golub, and Kiyomi, Emiko, and Issa Wilks. Some of you read drafts. Some of you just believed in me. I'm profoundly grateful to all of you.

I also want to thank the Society of Children's Book Writers and Illustrators. They are the heart and soul of children's book writing, and being a member has given me more than I can measure.

Thank you also to Anatole, who did not have a wart on his nose but who inspired this book nonetheless. Woof.

Finally, thank you to all my readers for sharing Peter's adventures with me. I hope that you find magic dogs of your own (and that you introduce me).

The Misadventures
of the
Magician's Dog

Prologue

That kid? Umm, really?

That's what I think the first time I see him. You would
have thought the same thing. I look in my magic water
bowl, and there he is, just beneath the surface of the
water, lying on his bed and reading. Hair buzzed close
to his scalp and round cheeks that still have a tinge of
babyish pink even though he's maybe twelve or thirteen.
Book held too close to his nose as if he needs glasses but
no one's noticed. Not fat, exactly, but sort of smooshy:
you know the type of kid I mean, the one who spends his
lunch hour in the library playing chess; who looks as if
he'd run and hide if a little adventure were to nip him on
his bottom. Nothing wrong with a kid like that—but me,
I need someone extraordinary. And this kid isn't it.

I eat a dog biscuit and keep watching because—let's
be honest—I'm pretty desperate. He reads for another half
hour, his expression never changing. Once he scratches
his belly, and once he sneezes. I've seen goldfish that
were more exciting.

I'm just considering drinking what's left of the water

1

in the bowl when, in the distance, a phone rings. The boy, hearing it, tenses: he marks his place in his book with his finger and sits up as if he's waiting. His door flies open. A girl, maybe ten, fills the empty space. "Peter, it's Dad! Come on!" Then she's gone.

But the boy—Peter, I now know—doesn't immediately follow. Instead, he waits a moment longer, his book clenched against his chest, his page lost. I try to understand what I'm seeing on his face as he stares at the spot where a moment before his sister stood. Excitement, anger, hurt, yearning? The emotions that flicker across his features seem too complex for a kid his age: a whole story unfolds in those few seconds, and it yanks at my heart in a way I don't expect.

Then he blinks, and his face settles once more into the empty passivity that it showed before. Only I now know how much is hiding behind it.

He stands up and walks out the door, not running like his sister. And for the first time in months, I feel a tiny spark of something that it takes me a minute to recognize as hope.

Maybe, I think, my tail thumping against the floor. *Just maybe.*

I eat another dog biscuit and keep watching.

Chapter One

The trouble started at dinner the night before Peter Lubinsky's twelfth birthday.

"Next week we have a field trip to the natural history museum," Peter's ten-year-old sister, Celia, announced as she plopped into her chair. That afternoon she'd spent her allowance on a package of feather hair extensions, and now pink and purple feathers dangled in her brown curls. "We've been studying dinosaurs in science, so we're going to look at dinosaur bones."

"They're called fossils," Peter said.

"Whatever," said Celia. "It'll be totally boring. But I need you to sign my permission slip, Mom, or I'll have to spend the day at the office."

Peter's mom served Celia a heaping portion of green beans. Then she put an equally generous helping on Peter's plate, nearly covering his meat loaf. "May I have green beans, please?" asked Isabelle, who was six.

"You can have mine," said Peter.

"Ha, ha," said his mother. "Here, Izzy."

"So can I go?" asked Celia.

"Go where?" asked their mom.

"To the museum. Weren't you listening?" Celia demanded.

Peter's mom sighed. "I'm sorry, honey. Of course you can go to the museum. I'm a little distracted—I'm still trying to figure out what we're going to do for Peter's birthday tomorrow."

Peter's face reddened. "I told you. I don't want to do anything."

"I know you don't want a proper party. But we have to celebrate somehow."

"I'd really rather not."

"But, Peter..."

"Ith addy omin ome or etey irthay?" Izzy asked through a mouthful of meat loaf.

"What?" said Peter.

"Swallow and ask again," said Peter's mother. "Talking with your mouth full is bad manners, honey."

"And besides, we can't understand a word you say," added Celia.

Izzy swallowed, then repeated, "Is Daddy coming home for Petey's birthday?"

Peter's mother's fork froze halfway to her mouth, and the skin suddenly seemed to stretch too tightly across the bones of her face. Still, she kept her smile pasted on—the one she had been wearing ever since Peter's father had left two months earlier for an unexpected deployment, his third in the past seven years.

"Daddy won't be home for Peter's birthday, Izzy," she said. "You remember. Daddy's fighting a war. He's doing it for our country, and that's why he can't be here right now."

"Maybe we could ask the war if he could come home for our birthdays," Izzy said. "Maybe the war doesn't know Peter's is tomorrow."

Celia's hands clenched the edge of the table. "Don't be dumb. You know Daddy won't be back for a long time. He told us when he left."

"He didn't say anything about birthdays," said Izzy.

"Well, duh. He didn't have to. He said he wouldn't be home for at least a year."

"Celia," Peter's mother said in a warning tone.

"What? She knows we can't see him."

"I just want to see him for our birthdays," said Izzy. "Birthdays are important."

"Well, you can't," said Celia. "Not even for birthdays."

"Celia's being mean, Mommy," Izzy said. "Will you make her stop? Please?"

"No," said Celia. "Make *her* stop."

Peter's mother pressed her fingers to her temples. "Enough, Celia. Your sister had a question, and she was trying to get it answered. She deserves our attention."

Celia opened her mouth as though she was going to argue, but instead she began to cry, angry sobs that filled the kitchen. Then Izzy started to cry, too, although hers were silent tears that trickled down her cheeks and puddled under her chin. Peter's mother just sat there, saying nothing, as if she had run out of words.

I have to say something, Peter thought. It wasn't a role he relished. Peter was the quiet one, the one who avoided

5

drama and conflict. He wasn't the one who spoke up in a crisis. *Say something,* he ordered himself as he watched the steam drift up from his green beans.

He opened his mouth, hoping words would just spill out.

"I know what I want for my birthday," he said.

It wasn't exactly a showstopper. No one even turned.

"I want a dog."

What had his mouth done? He hadn't meant to say the words and yet there they were, and he could do nothing to unspeak them.

His mother, Celia, and Izzy all gaped at him. Then Celia began to laugh. She laughed so hard that for a moment Peter was afraid she would choke and he would have to call 911.

"But, Peter!" she exclaimed, once she could speak. "You're scared to death of dogs!"

"I'm not scared of dogs," Peter lied.

"Oh, yes, you are," said Izzy, her tears forgotten. "Remember when we were out walking and that German shepherd wanted to play with us? You picked me up and carried me all the way home, even though I told you he was just being friendly."

"That dog might have hurt you," Peter said. "Did you see how big his teeth were? But I'm not scared of all dogs."

"Uh-huh. Right," said Celia.

"I'm not scared of dogs," Peter repeated. "Otherwise, why would I want one for my birthday?" He turned to his mother. *Say no,* his gaze begged; his mother didn't like dogs, either, and surely she was about to explain that a dog was too much responsibility and he was going to have to pick something else.

"Oh, Peter," she said, "really? I don't know. A dog is a lot of work...."

"Please?" begged Celia.

"Oh, please, please?" added Izzy.

Peter could see from his mother's expression that she was wavering. "It's really what you want for your birthday?" she asked.

From across the table, Celia's narrowed eyes challenged Peter to admit the truth.

"It's really what I want," he said.

Peter's mother smiled, and this time it was a genuine grin that erased the tiny lines of tension that usually crept from the corners of her eyes. "All right, then. Let's do it. Tomorrow morning after breakfast, we'll go to the dog rescue center and bring home the dog you like the best."

Izzy and Celia erupted at the news.

"What will we name him?" Celia demanded.

"What color will he be?" Izzy wondered.

Peter hoped their questions masked the fact that he himself had become very quiet.

That night in bed, Peter lay awake for hours, trying to figure out how he could avoid adopting a dog. He still didn't understand how those dreadful words had escaped from his mouth in the first place. Since they'd moved to Arizona last spring, he had often found himself saying the wrong things—to his mother, to Celia, to the kids at his new school, where his few attempts to make friends had failed miserably. But asking for a dog! That was something entirely different, and entirely worse.

Toward dawn he decided he had no choice: he needed to tell his mother and sisters he had changed his mind and he didn't want a dog after all. Celia would make fun of him, and Izzy would be disappointed. But at least he wouldn't have to have a dog.

He had just settled into an uneasy sleep when he heard his door swing open.

"Petey?"

"Yeah, Izzy?"

"Can I get in with you?"

"Yeah."

Izzy climbed in next to him. Her toes were tiny ice cubes against his knees.

"I wanted Daddy to come home today," she said.

"I know. I wish he could be here, too."

For a moment the room, shadowy in the early-morning light, was silent, and Peter wondered if Izzy had gone back to sleep.

"Why did he go back to the war?"

"I don't know. I guess because the air force told him to."

"A lot of the kids at school have dads who are at war, but the dads on TV always live with their kids," Izzy said.

"Families are different," said Peter. "That's just what Dad's job is. Flying planes for the air force, I mean."

Izzy's breathing slowed; Peter could tell she was settling down and that soon she really would be asleep.

"I'm glad you want a dog," she said, her voice sounding far away. "I know I'm going to love him. And I think...I hope he's going to like me, too."

"Go to sleep, Izzy," Peter said.

How bad could it be, having a dog? Peter asked his reflection in the window of the family's minivan the next morning. Most dogs did not bite their owners' fingers. Most dogs did not pee on their owners' possessions. Most dogs did not eat their owners' little sisters.

It could be bad, his reflection said. *With the luck you've been having, it could be sister-eating bad.*

It was clear to Peter what he ought to do. He ought to tell his mother to go back home so that they could celebrate his birthday by having too much cake and ice cream, like any normal family. But how could he tell her when every time he turned his head to speak, he saw Izzy perched on the seat behind him, her eyes shining? She looked happier than she had since their father had left.

He drummed his fingers against his knee and tried not to think of what was about to happen.

And then, more quickly than seemed possible, the minivan was pulling into a parking lot he'd never noticed before. The sign above the dusty stucco building said CANINE RESCUE CENTER, with the faded c, r, and c all painted white with black spots.

Peter's mom put the car into park. Then she turned to Peter. *She's going to ask me if I want to go through with this,* Peter thought. *What am I going to say?*

But she didn't ask. All she said was, "Let's go, honey."

Peter went.

Chapter Two

The first thing Peter noticed when he entered the Canine Rescue Center was the silence. He had expected dogs barking, but the only sound was the squeak of an overhead fan. In some ways, Peter found the lack of noise more eerie than he would have found barks and growls. Where were the dogs?

"Darn, darn, darn."

As one, Peter, his mother, and his sisters turned. The voice had come from a desk piled high with papers—a desk that had no one sitting behind it.

"C'mon," the voice wheedled now. "Just work. Please work. You know you want to." A series of sharp bangs followed.

Celia and Izzy started to giggle. "Umm...pardon me?" Peter's mom said, in her polite voice. "Is someone there?"

A frazzled-looking young man with a ponytail popped up from beneath the desk. "Oh! I didn't see you come in....Have you been waiting? I'm sorry. I take it you're here—of course you must be—for a dog?"

"I'm Grace Lubinsky," Peter's mother said, "and this is my son, Peter. Today's his birthday, and he wants to adopt a dog as his present."

"Wonderful!" the young man said. "We have so many extraordinary dogs here. I think you'll find... Well, it depends what you want.... But you'll find the perfect companion, I know."

Peter couldn't help himself. "What were you banging on?"

The young man sighed, and the enthusiasm left his face. "Oh. That. Well, the equipment here is all really old.... It's donated, you see. And it's not working, the computer. I thought... Well, I had just about given up, so banging seemed like... maybe not a good option, but an option."

"Would you, um, like me to look?"

"You know about computers? That would be... just excellent, truly excellent."

Peter slipped behind the desk. *You're procrastinating,* his mind told him, but Peter didn't care. He liked computers, and he didn't like dogs. Facing him, the monitor was black and lifeless. Peter reached over and pressed the power button on the computer. Nothing. Then he checked the cord in the back, running his fingers down its length until he felt an unexpected rough spot.

"Here's your problem," he said, feeling more cheerful than he had all day. "It's the power cord. It's been chewed on."

"Rusty!" said the young man, snapping his fingers, as though this explained everything.

"Uh...," said Peter. "It's not actually rusty. It's been chewed on. I mean, with teeth."

The young man laughed, then patted Peter's shoulder. "No, no—Rusty is a dog. I had him out here with me yesterday. That rascal—he'd chew through anything. I should've checked the cord; I just didn't think..."

One more disadvantage of dogs, Peter thought. "You can get a new power cord at any electronics store," he said. "They don't cost that much."

"Thank you so much," said the young man. "Really, thank you. I'm Timothy, by the way. I would have... Well, anything you need, please let me know."

"Well, right now we need a dog," Peter's mom reminded Timothy. She was smiling, clearly pleased that Peter had been able to help, but Izzy, waiting next to her, was wiggling with impatience, and Celia was restlessly shifting her weight from foot to foot.

"Oh, yes, right," said Timothy. He hurried to a door in the opposite wall. "They're through here," he said, pushing the door open. An explosion of barking immediately filled the office. He had been wrong, Peter thought; eerie silence was better than noise. "Let me know when you find one you like," Timothy continued. "And if you don't want your cords chewed on...maybe not Rusty."

Celia and Izzy didn't need a second invitation. They were off like shots. Peter, his heart thumping unpleasantly, lingered by his mother's side.

"Go on, honey," she said. "I'm going to get the paperwork started."

He had no choice. He walked through the door.

The long room he entered was filled with dogs. Everywhere Peter looked, he saw dark eyes, staring at him expectantly. The air smelled of urine and wet fur, and the open-topped steel cages offered little reassurance.

"This one is so cute! Peter, you have to see her!" exclaimed Celia.

Peter thought about Izzy's dreamy voice that morning as she drifted off to sleep, how happy she'd sounded talking about a dog. If there was one person in the world he wanted to be happy, it was Izzy—Izzy, who had always been small and quiet but had somehow gotten smaller and quieter in the eight weeks since their father had left. Peter and Celia at least remembered their father's other deployments, but Izzy had been only three when he'd come back the last time. When their father had met them at the airport that day, he'd ruffled Peter's hair, pressed Celia to his chest, then swung Izzy high into the air before clutching her against him. "Now I'm back for good," he'd said, and Peter could have sworn he'd seen tears in his father's eyes—his father, who never cried. Remembering those tears somehow made Peter feel braver now, and he straightened his back and walked over to where Celia knelt in front of a cage. There was nothing to do but choose a dog fast and get out.

"Her name is Beauty," Celia said. "That's what it says on her cage, anyway. Isn't she just perfect?"

"Umm . . . Sure," said Peter, looking at the glossy black dog, who was sniffing at Celia's hand. Just standing this close made Peter sweat—or maybe it was the lack of air-conditioning. "I guess."

"Will you choose her?"

Just then Beauty glanced up at him and *woof*ed. Peter jumped backward.

"Let me look around a bit more," he said.

The next cage over held three orangeish-red puppies. They scrambled rambunctiously at the sight of Peter, climbing over and under each other in an attempt to reach him. No. The cage after that held a sleeping yellow dog. Peter appreciated the fact that the dog was sleeping, but he was also too large. The terrier in the next cage growled at Peter.

In the next cage, he found Izzy. She was sitting on the floor between a ratty towel and a half-chewed dog treat. A small brown dog was limp in her lap. The sign outside the cage said TEDDY.

"Isn't he cute?" she breathed.

"How did you get in there?" Peter asked, struggling to keep his voice calm. He didn't want to startle the dog.

Izzy frowned. "I couldn't open the door. I had to climb."

"I think they lock the cages on purpose. So the dogs stay in and the people stay out."

"Oh. Do you think I need to get out now?"

"I really think you should. You never know if a dog might bite."

Izzy looked down at the dog sprawled over her, his eyes half closed and his breath rattling out in a soft snore. "He's nice. He won't bite me." Still, Izzy gently placed Teddy on the ratty towel, then pulled herself up the side of the cage. Peter caught her as she came down.

He squeezed her harder than he should have, half in relief and half in frustration.

"Please don't go in any more cages," he said.

"Will you adopt him?" Izzy asked. "I think he'd be a really good pet."

Peter studied the dog his sister had been holding. *At least he's small,* he thought—not much bigger than a loaf of bread. And he looked gentle enough, lying there on the rag. He kind of resembled an oversized guinea pig.

"Maybe," he said. "Let me think about it, okay? You want to walk with me and look at more dogs?"

"Sure," said Izzy, but a moment later, Peter's mom entered the room, and Izzy darted off to show Teddy to her.

Peter forced himself to look at the rest of the dogs, but he couldn't help dismissing all of them. *I guess it's going to be Izzy's dog,* he thought.

Then he got to the last cage. It was set apart from the others at the end of the long room. While the other cages just had walls, this one had mesh over the top, too, and three separate locks on the door. *Must be a fierce one,* Peter thought, *to have so many locks.* He started to move away.

"I want that one," a boy's voice said.

Peter looked around in confusion to see who had spoken.

"This dog," the voice insisted. "This one is perfect."

"Wonderful!" said his mother, hurrying over to Peter's side.

"Really?" said Celia.

"He's . . . I guess he's cute," said Izzy.

"Who said that?" asked Peter.

"Who said what?" asked Peter's mom.

"Who said they wanted this dog?"

"Why, you did, honey. Do you not want that dog?"

And the voice spoke again, and Peter now recognized it as his own, and he could even feel his own mouth moving, only he knew—he knew!—that he wasn't the one doing the talking. "This is the dog," his voice said. "This is the dog I want for my birthday."

Peter's hands rose up to his mouth. But short of gagging himself, there was nothing he could do to stop the voice. Should he argue with it? he wondered. But his mother was already looking at him strangely; if he denied saying those words when he had clearly been the one speaking, she would think he was crazy. They would *all* think he was crazy.

Maybe he *was* crazy.

His mother left to get Timothy. His sisters stood next to him, staring down into the cage with all the locks. It occurred to Peter that he ought to look at the dog, too, and for the first time he let his eyes move past the cage to its occupant.

The dog inside was . . . well, calling him scruffy would be generous.

His fur was dirty white. His legs were short, but his body was long; he looked like a big dog with a short dog's legs. His ears stood straight up from his head like a jackrabbit's, his beard was going gray, and his long, pointed nose had what seemed to be a wart on one side. His tail, which ended in a rather magnificent plume, was his only redeeming feature. As Peter watched, he began to lick his bottom.

To make matters worse, Peter could tell that Celia was just barely holding in giggles. "Peter, are you sure about this?" she asked.

"No!" Peter wanted to shout, but his mouth was once more in control. "Yes," it answered. "I think he's beautiful."

Celia collapsed in laughter.

Enough already, mouth, Peter thought in despair.

His mom returned, Timothy following her. Timothy's eyes widened in surprise when he saw which cage they were standing in front of.

"You want to adopt *this* dog?" he asked.

At least this time Peter expected what was coming. "Yes," answered his mouth.

"Hmm... Well... This dog, huh?"

Peter's mom got to the point. "Timothy, why are there so many locks on the dog's cage? Is he dangerous?"

Timothy dropped to his knees and held out his hand to the dog, who promptly came over to sniff it. "Oh, no, he's not dangerous," Timothy said, "not in the least. It wouldn't be right, you know, to offer a dangerous dog for adoption. This guy, he's actually as smart as they come, and a really nice fellow to boot. Sometimes... well, sometimes it seems like he understands every word I say. In fact..." Timothy paused, and, watching him, Peter got the distinct feeling that there was something in particular he wanted to tell them. But the words must have stuck in his throat, because after a minute he shook his head a little, and when he finally continued, Peter could tell he had switched topics. "Someone left him in a carrier outside our front door a few days back, and it turns out he's a bit of an escape artist, that's all. Locks come undone around him. Cages fall apart. Five times he's gotten out already. Every time we find him in a different spot. In the hallway. In with another dog. Once we even found him in the bathroom."

"Oh, dear," said Peter's mother.

"I still want him," said Peter's mouth.

Timothy looked at Peter's mom, then scratched his head. "Hmm. What about this? What if you fostered this dog—that's kind of like a temporary adoption, so it'll give you a chance to see what you think. Give it a week or so. If he's the right dog for you, then, well, that's wonderful. As I said, he's a nice, smart guy, so if he stays put, you'll have yourself a terrific pet. And if he's determined to escape...we've got a lot of great dogs here. You can always choose somebody who suits you better."

"I think it's a reasonable idea. Peter, what do you think?"

Peter waited to see what his mouth would have to say. When it didn't answer, he nodded mutely. What else could he do? At least if he was fostering the dog, he could tell his mother at the end of a week that he didn't want to keep him.

That is, assuming his mouth worked at the end of the week.

Assuming they all survived the week.

Chapter Three

That evening, Peter perched miserably on the far side of the bed, staring down at The Dog.

He called him that because his new dog didn't yet have a name. Celia had asked Timothy what the dog rescue people called him, and Timothy shrugged. "Pretty much all the dogs here have names. But nothing's stuck to him yet. Maybe you'll have better luck than we have."

Celia had spent all afternoon suggesting possibilities. She thought maybe Jack, because the dog's ears stood up like a jackrabbit's, or Pinocchio, because he had such a long nose. Izzy proposed Darling, because he was such a sweet dog; you could just tell, couldn't you?

In fact, Peter couldn't. He didn't actually care what they named The Dog, since with any luck he would be gone soon enough. Peter would have named him Darling just to please Izzy, except that he couldn't bring himself to actually say "Darling" when he was looking at The Dog. "Maybe I'll call you Not Darling," he said now from where he sat on the bed, and the attempt at humor made him feel just the tiniest bit better. It helped that it was hard to imagine being eaten alive by somebody named Not Darling. "So tell me, Not Darling, how did you do that trick in the rescue center? The one where you made me say I wanted to take you home? Because either I'm going crazy, or someone played a trick on me. And I don't think I'm crazy, I really don't. I feel pretty much the way I've always felt, only maybe a little older, I guess, now that I'm twelve."

He glanced at his clock—it was almost eight. He was twelve years and thirteen hours old. He didn't quite believe it, because today hadn't felt like a birthday. He had spent all evening both hoping for and dreading his father's call, but the phone never rang; instead his father emailed, the way he did most days. Peter had reread that email enough times that he had it memorized.

Dear Peter,
    Happy birthday, son! Hope it's a special day. Wish I could have been there for a game of chess. Gotta run, but I'm thinking about you. Tell your mom and sisters I love them.
                                          Love, Dad

Peter hadn't answered. He rarely replied to his father's emails, because he couldn't figure out what to say. Sometimes he just wrote,

Hi, Dad. I'm good. Hope you are, too.

That was at least enough so that he could say yes when his mother asked if he'd written back. Otherwise, she would tilt her head and purse her lips, a look of concern on her face that was infinitely worse than a scolding. But he hated sending those short emails. It was kind of lie, wasn't it? To say you were good when you weren't? Peter often wondered whether his father hit Delete immediately after reading his emails, seeing no need to save words that said nothing. Peter always saved his dad's emails, even when they were only a sentence or two long. They sat there in Peter's in-box, and sometimes he would reread them all, one after another, two months' worth of short notes about the weather and the food, and the occasional description of a city his father had visited.

The Dog was still sitting there, staring at him and panting. Peter wished The Dog would go to sleep and leave him alone. He found those watchful eyes demanding—as if The Dog wanted him to do or say something. "You know, a tiny part of me was actually excited about adopting a dog," Peter told The Dog now. "I mean, I really don't like dogs. I've never liked dogs. But I thought... some part of me thought maybe I could find a dog that was different. A dog that wasn't so... doggy. And maybe..." Peter stopped. The Dog was, after all, just a dog, and it didn't matter what Peter said to him. But if he kept talking, if he said aloud that he had hoped that at the rescue center he might end up finding an actual, well, *friend,* he thought the sadness that he kept pushed down in his chest might float up and engulf him, and then where would he be? "And instead I got you. Not Darling. The doggiest dog of all. And now we have to stay together for a whole week—unless, that is, I get lucky and you run away."

"Well, gee," said The Dog. He yawned, showing off a long pink tongue and a wicked set of incisors. "Way to make a guy feel welcome. Really."

Peter froze.

"Aren't you going to say anything?" asked The Dog. His voice was gravelly, somewhere between a bark and a normal human voice, but his words were perfectly clear. "Aren't you going to tell me how much you wish I weren't here? I mean, I wasn't expecting steak and caviar or anything—not that I would mind a steak, if you have one—but I've been here less than eight hours, and you're already counting the minutes until I go."

"Dogs don't talk," said Peter. He touched his forehead to see if he had a fever, but his skin was cool. Desperate, he looked around his room, but the empty bookshelves and the half-unpacked boxes that his mother had been asking him to deal with for months didn't offer any answers.

"You sound pretty sure of yourself," said The Dog. "But how exactly do you know dogs don't talk? I mean, here I am, talking to you, after all."

"Everyone knows dogs don't talk!" Peter said. "It's just a fact."

The Dog snorted. "Can I give you some advice? Don't let other people tell you what's possible or impossible."

"Can you just give me a minute?" Peter asked. "To think about this?"

"Sure," said The Dog. "My ear itches, anyway."

The Dog scratched his ear. And Peter thought. The Dog might be sarcastic, Peter realized, but he was also patient. He let Peter think as long as he wanted.

It was maybe five minutes later when Peter s
"Okay."

"Yes?" drawled The Dog.

"I've been trying to think about this logically," said Peter, taking a deep breath. "And I know for a fact that most dogs don't speak. And since you do, I'm pretty sure you're not an ordinary dog."

"That seems like a reasonable conclusion," said The Dog. Perhaps it was Peter's imagination, but The Dog's posture seemed a little less condescending than it had—or maybe it was just that one of his ears had turned inside out. "Tell me more."

"I think you made me adopt you," said Peter. "Something made me adopt you, anyway, and who else would but you? So that means you have some sort of powers, too. What I want to know is if you're really a dog. And whoever you are, what it is you want from me."

"Well," said The Dog, "now you're asking good questions, at least. In answer to your first question, yes, I am a dog. Really, truly a dog, born to a dog mother and destined to die a dog death."

"So how did you...?"

"How did I make you take me home? And how come I can talk? That's a little more complicated. I'm an ordinary dog, but I haven't had an ordinary life. Up until about a month ago"—The Dog paused for dramatic effect—"I was a magician's assistant."

Peter laughed.

The Dog looked hurt. "Why are you laughing?"

Peter would have answered, but he couldn't stop laughing. It was strange, because he couldn't remember last time something had struck him as funny, and he wasn't even sure this *was* funny, but it made him laugh anyway. The idea of a talking dog was bad enough. The idea of a dog—of this scruffy, ugly dog!—as a magician's assistant was ridiculous.

The Dog watched him for a minute, then growled. "Fine. Don't believe me." As Peter's laughter turned to hiccups, The Dog closed his eyes. And suddenly he wasn't there anymore.

Instead, in the middle of Peter's carpet stood an eight-foot-tall greenish-blue dragon, its wings folded tight against its back so it could fit in the room. A dragon with a wart on the side of its nose. A dragon that stretched its neck toward Peter, put its face right in front of Peter's face, and roared.

Peter screamed, but no sound came out.

He was catching his breath to scream again when the dragon disappeared, replaced once more by The Dog.

"Peter, did you hear that?" called Peter's mom from the living room.

"P...P...Plane," Peter answered, but his voice was still too quiet for his mom to hear. He cleared his throat. "I think it was a plane," he repeated. "Over the house. It roared."

"Oh. Thanks."

The Dog was lounging on the floor with a smug look on his long face.

"You were a magician's assistant?" Peter asked, his voice quivering only slightly.

"Uh-huh."

"And you know how to do magic?"

"Uh-huh."

Peter rubbed his eyes, then glanced above The Dog to the spot where a moment before the dragon had stood. His heart was racing so fast it felt as if his chest might explode. He ought to be terrified, and he was. But he felt something else, too, something that took him by surprise.

"How did you do it?" he asked.

"The magician taught me," The Dog said.

Peter wasn't sure where the words he said next came from. They weren't the sort of words he would have imagined he would ever say. Maybe it was because this all felt so unreal. Maybe it was because today was his birthday, and if magic things were going to happen, weren't they more likely to happen on this day than on any other? "Can you teach me?"

The Dog's ears shot up. "How did you...That was actually what I was planning to do. Teach you magic, I mean. Seeing as it's your birthday and all."

Peter felt a shiver climb his spine. He couldn't imagine why The Dog was offering such an amazing gift; all he knew was that he wanted The Dog to teach him quickly, before he chickened out or The Dog changed his mind. "You will? Really? When?"

"Why not now?" said The Dog, standing up and wagging his plumy tail.

Chapter Four

Peter told his mother he was going to bed. This was The Dog's suggestion. He said learning magic might take a while, and it would be better if they were left alone.

"So early?" said Peter's mother, glancing at her watch. "It's not even nine yet."

Peter faked a yawn. "I'm pretty tired."

Peter's mother yawned as well, and her yawn wasn't faked. "I guess I'm tired, too. But I've got another twenty papers to grade tonight." Peter's mother taught history at a nearby high school; she had been lucky to find a job, she told Peter, but he knew she missed her old school district in New Jersey, where his father's last base had been. They had spent two years there, the longest Peter had ever lived in one place in his life.

"Listen, Peter," his mother said, pushing her reading glasses up so that they rested on top of her head. "I wanted to ask you—was it a good birthday?"

"It was great," said Peter. "Thanks for the cake. And the new video game, too."

"And the dog?" his mother asked. Thin lines of worry formed between her brows.

"Thank you especially for The Dog," said Peter, and he sounded as though he meant it, even to his own ears. He still didn't quite believe that any of this was real, but if it was a dream, he didn't think he wanted to wake up—not yet, anyway. "I know he's…well, he's going to make life more interesting, anyway."

"I'm glad," Peter's mother said. She leaned forward to kiss Peter lightly on his forehead, and he smelled the citrus scent of her shampoo mixed with the sharp tang of the mint tea she'd been drinking. They were his favorite smells, the ones he'd been breathing all his life. "I know it was hard this year, having your dad gone and all. You were really brave about it."

"I'm not brave," said Peter. "I'm scared of more things than anyone."

"You're brave in the ways that count," said his mother. "And today—well, today you adopted a dog!"

"I guess," said Peter.

"Sweet dreams," said Peter's mother.

"Thanks," said Peter, and he headed back to his room.

The next magic The Dog did was to make three pillows and a stuffed animal look like a sleeping Peter and a sleeping Dog. "Put them there," The Dog told Peter. "That's right. Close to each other on the bed."

"My mom would never believe I'd let you sleep near me," Peter objected.

The Dog snorted. "Don't worry: when it comes time

to actually go to bed, I'll find a nice spot on the floor. But if the illusions are close together, I can do one spell instead of two, and illusions can be tricky to maintain if you're not next to them. And your mom will probably think it's cute that we're sleeping next to each other."

"Was it an illusion when you changed into a dragon?"

The Dog gave the dog equivalent of a shrug. "Maybe. But I could turn into a real dragon if I wanted to."

Peter wanted to ask more about this, but before he could, The Dog focused his attention once again on the bed. Peter wasn't sure exactly what he expected to happen next: incantations, tail waving, something grandiose. Instead, The Dog closed his eyes and gritted his teeth as if he were taking a poop.

Peter leaned over to check the carpet, just in case. When he looked back, The Dog was grinning wickedly. And there on the bed was another dog, and next to him another Peter.

"Wow," said Peter. He could even see his own chest rising and falling as he breathed.

The Dog tilted his head at a cocky angle. "Nice work, huh? They won't last forever, though, so we'd better get going."

Peter went to the window and very quietly pulled it open, then lifted out the screen. The Dog immediately leapt through, while Peter followed more slowly. He put the screen back so none of the neighbors would notice. Then he looked around for The Dog.

"Arrooo!" echoed from down the street. And then again, *"Arrooo!"*

Peter started off toward the sound.

It was a beautiful night. Peter did not in general like the weather in Arizona: the hot days of the previous summer had left him sticky and miserable, and even in September and October, it had been too warm for him to enjoy being outdoors. But nighttime was another story. Once the sun set, the desert cooled off, the darkness seemingly absorbing the heat. Tonight, Peter felt almost cold as he hurried down the sidewalk, and for a moment he wished he had changed out of his shorts and into jeans. The street was empty except for him, and through the windows of the passing houses, each identical to his own, he could see the blue flickers of televisions; it was easy enough to imagine his neighbors parked on their couches, remotes in their hands. They were inside, staring at screens, all of them the same as the others, and he was out here, in the night, following a magic dog. He sucked the cool night air into his lungs, astounded by his own daring.

"*Arrooooo!*" The Dog howled again. He stalked out from the shadow of a cactus. "There you are. Finally. What took you so long?"

Peter didn't bother to answer. "Where are we going?"

"Someplace private," The Dog said. He turned right at the end of the block, Peter following. A few houses later, he turned right again.

"Here," he said finally, his beard bobbing in satisfaction.

"The golf course?" Peter asked in confusion.

"The golf course," repeated The Dog.

*   *   *

The first thing The Dog did was pee on the green. His urine ran down the flag and into the hole.

"Gross," said Peter.

"It's not gross," said The Dog. "It's friendly. Like leaving a note when you visit a friend who's not home. It's letting them know I was here."

"Pee is not the same as a note," said Peter.

"It is if you're a dog," said The Dog.

Peter sighed. "I still don't understand why we're here. Why the golf course?"

"It's private," answered The Dog. "It's quiet. It has a lot of open space. And I've always wanted to pee in one of those holes. So are you ready to get started?"

Peter shivered. He didn't know whether or not it was from the cold. "Yes."

"This is the thing about magic," The Dog said. "It's really just a question of using your brain in a way that you don't normally use it. For example, if you weren't ever taught to read, then that would be a capability of your brain that you weren't using. Magic is kind of like that."

"So anyone can do magic?" Peter asked. "I mean, if they're taught?"

"It's not quite as straightforward as that," The Dog replied, raising his nose to sniff experimentally at the breeze. "My old master had this theory. You know how some people are able to do incredibly complex math in their heads, without calculators? Or to compose music from a very young age? Well, it's the same with magic, which comes naturally for some people and doesn't for others. The only difference is that most people are able to learn to perform math or music

30

to some degree, while only a few people—a very, very few people—are able to learn to do magic at all."

This all sounded rather complicated to Peter. But he understood what The Dog was saying clearly enough that his mood immediately plummeted. "So you're one of the few who are able to use their brains to do magic?"

"Me? Of course not. I'm a dog, not a human. I can do magic because the magician wished it."

"Oh."

"Why so glum?" The Dog asked after a moment.

"If only a very, very few people can learn to do magic, what makes you think I can?"

The Dog wagged his tail. "Let's just say I've got a feeling about you. And it helps that you're a kid. All good magicians learn when they're young. After a certain age, inflexibility starts to settle in."

"All right," said Peter. He still felt dubious—he was a good enough student, but he had never thought of himself as particularly adept at using his brain—but it seemed worth trying. "So what do I do?"

"Bend down," said The Dog.

"What?"

"Bend down," The Dog growled.

Peter bent down.

The Dog's face was suddenly close to Peter's. His damp nose nuzzled through Peter's hair, and Peter couldn't help envisioning himself minus an ear. "Here," said The Dog, tapping his nose against Peter's scalp. The spot was about two inches behind Peter's right temple. "This is the part of your brain you have to use to do magic. Just think about what you want, but think with that part."

"How do you think with a particular part of your brain? Don't people just, well, think?"

The Dog snorted, his warm, stinky breath ruffling Peter's hair. "Are we going to do this or not?"

"We're going to do this," said Peter.

"Well, then, I'm telling you—think about what you want, but with that part of your brain!"

Peter didn't say anything for a moment.

"What are you waiting for now?" asked The Dog.

"It's just... what do you mean, what I want?"

The Dog sighed. "If you're going to do magic, Peter, you have to want something. To be rich. To be invisible. To be able to fly." He stared at Peter, really stared at him, hard. "You must know what you want, right? That's why you asked me to teach you."

As the breeze whispered through the orange trees surrounding them, Peter thought about The Dog's question. It wasn't something anyone normally asked him. But here it was, his birthday, and he was being granted a wish. *Flying,* he thought. Once, when Peter was eight, his father had borrowed a friend's Cessna and taken Peter for what he'd called a spin. Peter had loved diving through the sky as the clouds parted in wisps before them, his father next to him. Imagine how it would feel without the plane! Now Peter tried to think about flying with that particular spot on his head. He tried and tried. Nothing happened.

"Try again," ordered The Dog.

"Maybe it would help if you showed me," said Peter. "I wasn't really watching when you did it before."

Staring downward, The Dog gritted his teeth, and

Peter thought he was going to refuse. Instead, one moment there was a twig on the ground, and the next the twig was gone and in its place was a bone. A bone that The Dog immediately began to gnaw.

"Wow," said Peter. "That's so cool. Does it taste like a real...?"

The Dog put the bone down on the green. "Your turn. If you think you've had enough show-and-tell, I mean." He cocked his head. "Or maybe you're too scared to learn it after all."

In general, Peter was a pretty easygoing kid. He knew, for instance, that Celia was embarrassed by him: by his shyness, by his love of computers and space and books, by his outcast status in the seventh grade. Celia was, well, Celia: after only two months at their new school, she was already the girl everyone wanted to sit next to at lunch. Merely by existing, Peter disappointed Celia, and he couldn't blame her for not letting him forget it. If Celia made fun of him, so be it. But The Dog was another story. Peter hadn't chosen to be with The Dog; The Dog had, in fact, forced himself upon Peter. And now The Dog was insulting him.

It made Peter mad. Mad enough that, staring at The Dog's snarky face, he made up his mind that he was going to do magic, if only to show The Dog: not only was he going to do magic, he would do magic *to* The Dog.

So Peter thought. He thought as hard as he could with that particular spot on his head that The Dog had showed him.

When he looked down, The Dog was gone. On the ground in front of Peter was the bone, looking particularly savage against the civilized green of the golf course's grass. And sure enough, when he knelt next to the bone, there, growing in that perfect grass, was a small gray mushroom. Elongated so that it looked just a bit like a dog, with a hint of a plumy tail. Triumph flooded through Peter. He had done it! Done magic! All he had to do was think with that one spot and anything was possible: wasn't that the sort of power every kid dreamed of? Magic even had a taste, he realized; it was a little like chocolate, a little like cherries, and a little like something rich and old that he couldn't quite put his finger on.

Maybe, he thought, power tasted like a sort of mushroom.

Ha ha.

So now he knew how to do magic: what next? He was eager to try it again. Something simple, he thought. The Dog had turned a twig into a bone. What if Peter turned a leaf into a cheeseburger? He picked up a leaf from the ground, held it in his hand, and thought with that particular part of his brain.

Nothing happened.

He tried again.

Nothing happened.

He felt the first cold edge of panic but pushed the feeling down. He would just have to turn The Dog back so that The Dog could show him what he was doing wrong. He had been planning to turn The Dog back, anyway; he shouldn't have lost his temper.

And that was when the panic turned into a sinking feeling that started someplace in his throat and ended in his stomach. If he couldn't turn a leaf into a cheese-burger, would he be able to turn the mushroom back into The Dog? He had turned The Dog into a plant. No, worse than a plant: a fungus. And he might not be able to change him back.

"Umm, Dog? Are you . . . are you in there?"

If The Dog was in there, he chose not to answer. *Of course,* Peter reminded himself, *mushrooms don't have mouths.*

"I'm sorry," Peter said, a little bit lamely, just in case The Dog could hear him. "I'll turn you back in just a minute. Really. I just need to . . ." What he needed to do was figure out what he had done so he could undo it. But how? There was no room for screwing up now. If Peter didn't figure out how to fix this, he would end up, in effect, having taken a life, because there was no doubt in his mind that come tomorrow morning, this little mushroom growing on the putting green would be efficiently removed by who-ever was in charge of mowing, trimming, and beautifying the base's golf course.

Above Peter, the sky sparkled with stars, but now that he was alone, the golf course seemed dark and strangely silent. In the distance, he could still hear the occasional sounds of cars, but they felt as far away from him now as yesterday seemed from today—yesterday, when he was eleven, before he had known about magicians or talking dogs or that special part of his brain. That spot. Peter tried to remember the feeling of The Dog's muzzle against his head. There. No, there. Pressing his finger to his scalp, he squinted down at the mushroom. *Turn into a dog,* he thought as fiercely as he could. That wasn't quite right. *Turn into The Dog. Turn into The Dog. Turn into The Dog!*

Please turn into The Dog?

But it was no good. The mushroom was nothing but a mushroom.

Peter moved his finger a little to the left and tried again. And again. And again.

Peter didn't wear a watch, so he had no idea how long he had been crouching on the golf course when he finally gave up. All he knew was that he'd poked himself in the head so many times his scalp felt like a pincushion. He was exhausted, and everything was blurring. A cold breeze blew in from the desert. Goose bumps climbed his arms.

It was then that a solution came to him. It wasn't, admittedly, a perfect plan. Too many things could go wrong. On the other hand, it offered at least some hope that when the sun rose, Peter wouldn't be standing in exactly this spot, waiting for the golf course's keepers to throw him out.

Biting his lower lip, Peter walked to the nearby grove of orange trees and, in the darkness, searched the grass beneath them. When he couldn't find what he needed, he reached up and broke a small branch from the shortest of the trees. Then he hurried back to the mushroom, its location made obvious by the bone.

Using the branch as a shovel, Peter began to dig.

He didn't know how long a mushroom's roots were, so he dug a circle perhaps eight inches in diameter and another five inches deep. The hardest part was digging under the mushroom. If he'd had a spade, Peter could have just slipped it beneath the roots and pushed the ball of dirt from the ground. Since all he had was a stick, he had to slide it back and forth and back again, cutting through dirt clods and grass roots and who knew what else. He tried not to think about worms wriggling help-lessly as he sliced them in half.

When the ground finally seemed loose enough, he stuck both his hands down into the earth, spread his fin-gers wide, and pulled. At first the dirt resisted him. But just as he was about to ease out his hands and pick up his stick once again, something in the ground released. Just like that, the mushroom was in his grasp, unbeliev-ably still intact, and in the middle of the once-perfect green was a raggedy hole.

He took off his shirt and wrapped the mess of dirt and roots and grass and mushroom in it. As an after-thought, he added the bone. Then he started for home.

Chapter Five

Peter woke to Izzy's small face, inches from his own. Her gaze was panicked. "Peter! Peter!" she said. "Oh, please wake up, Peter!"

"What is it?" he asked, but he already knew.

"The Dog is gone!"

"What do you mean?"

"I've looked all over," she said. "I can't find him anywhere!"

Peter glanced at his clock. It was 5:17, which meant he'd been asleep for only two hours. Then he checked the mattress next to him and breathed a sigh of relief. Last night, when he had crept back in through his window, he'd almost yelped at the sight of himself and The Dog sleeping peacefully in his bed—in the hours he'd spent on the golf course, he'd forgotten about The Dog's illusion. Not knowing what else to do, he'd hidden the mushroom in a shoe box in his closet, then pushed the pillows aside and climbed right onto the image of his sleeping self, which thankfully had no more substance than the flickering light from a movie projector. If the illusion was still there in the morning, he'd thought, he'd deal with it then.

But perhaps moving the pillows had disrupted The Dog's magic, or perhaps the illusion had just disappeared as The Dog had warned: either way, the image was now gone.

"Do you know where he is?" asked Izzy. "Should I wake up Mommy and Celia?"

"He was in the room when I went to sleep," said Peter. (This was true, strictly speaking, if you counted being in the closet as being in the room.)

Izzy brightened. "He must be hiding, then. You and I can look for him!"

"Umm...I guess..."

"Let's start with the living room!"

Peter and Izzy spent the next thirty minutes searching the house, Peter feeling guiltier with every passing moment. They peered behind furniture, inside cabinets, beneath rugs—Peter agreed to anything Izzy suggested, no matter how unlikely. All the while, he was thinking furiously, replaying the events of the previous evening. In his head, he kept hearing The Dog's voice asking what he wanted. Last night, he had thought that what he wanted most was to fly. But now, as he and Izzy tiptoed around their house, he realized that wasn't what he really wanted. What he really wanted was to bring his father home.

Today was Sunday. On Sunday mornings, Peter's father always made pancakes—daddycakes, Izzy called them. The smell of hot oil and warm maple syrup would fill the house as Peter and his sisters stood around the stove, calling out suggestions. A rose with a long stem. A stick-figure girl in a dress. A space shuttle about to take flight. Whatever the request, Peter's father would carefully ladle batter into the pan as though it were paint being brushed onto a canvas. Then Peter, Celia, and Izzy would giggle as his delicate lines ballooned in the skillet, the girl's head growing puffy and enormous, the rose transformed into a blob of oversized petals.

"Vat has happened to my art?" Peter's father exclaimed, in an accent that sometimes sounded Russian and sometimes French. "That ees not the way I drew it!"

They were none of them whole without his father: not Peter, not his mother, not his sisters. Their lives might look the same from the outside, but they themselves weren't the same; and the differences were made worse because they all knew that their father's absence might not be temporary; that he could come back hurt, or not come back at all. They had lived on air force bases all their lives. Even Izzy realized what could happen to parents who went to war.

And then The Dog had come. What The Dog had offered, Peter realized, was a way to ensure his father's safety. And how had Peter responded? By losing his temper and turning The Dog into a mushroom.

Last night Peter had felt desperate to fix his mistake merely because it seemed the moral thing to do. If you turned someone into a mushroom, you ought to turn him back. Today...well, today more selfish reasons had intruded. If Peter could return The Dog to his former self, perhaps The Dog would forgive him and teach him how to use magic to bring his father home. What Peter needed now was to get back to his room and try to do magic once more. But to do that, he would have to slip away from Izzy.

"I saw his tail," she reported after peeking under Celia's closed door. "It swished out from under the bed, and then it went back in."

"That must have been a sock," whispered Peter. The last thing he needed was for Izzy to wake up Celia. Celia always made things more complicated.

"Socks don't swish," said Izzy.

"How could he be in Celia's room?" Peter asked. "Celia sleeps with her door closed. He couldn't get in."

"He could if she got up to pee," said Izzy. "And she almost always gets up to pee. I hear her in the middle of the night."

Peter looked down at his sister in her pink-and-white-striped pajamas with her blond hair sticking up from her head. "Why are you awake in the middle of the night?" he asked.

Izzy stared at her toes and shrugged.

"Seriously, Izzy," Peter said. "I know you wake up early, and that's why you get in with me, but I didn't know you were awake in the night, too. What's going on?"

Izzy still refused to meet his eyes.

"Kids need sleep," Peter said. "Are you staying up worrying? Is that what it is? Is it... is it because of Dad?"

"Is what because of Dad?"

Peter and Izzy had been whispering. But Celia must not have been sleeping that deeply, or else her unerring desire to be where she was least wanted had pulled her awake. Whatever the cause, when Peter—startled—turned around, there she was, leaning against the doorframe, her arms crossed over her nightshirt and her eyes narrowed and curious. One of her feathers from the day before had come loose from her hair; it now balanced precariously on her shoulder.

"Nothing," Peter said. "Nothing is because of Dad."

"Did The Dog come into your room in the night?" Izzy asked.

Celia glanced at the messy room behind her. "No."

"I think I saw his tail under your bed," Izzy said, and she darted past Celia, skipping over piles of laundry and stuffed animals and nail polishes to peer behind the purple dust ruffle that hid Celia's mattress. Izzy's head emerged a moment later, her expression bleak. "Oh," she said, sinking back onto her heels and looking as though she might cry. "He's not here, either. Where is he?"

"What's going on?" said Celia. "The Dog is missing?"

Peter swallowed. "He disappeared in the night. Nobody's sure where he is." Well, Peter couldn't be *sure* he was still in the shoe box in the closet, since he hadn't checked recently, right?

Celia, whose attention had been on Izzy, froze, then turned until she was staring straight at Peter's face. "What do you mean, he disappeared?"

Peter tried to look innocent and worried at the same time. "I mean he disappeared," he repeated. "He was there when I went to sleep and gone when I woke up. We've been looking for him ever since."

Celia studied Peter's face for a moment longer, then shook her head disapprovingly, her brown curls bouncing. "Peter Lubinsky, you are such a liar."

Peter could feel his fragile control over the situation slipping.

Izzy had been poking through Celia's room haphazardly, probably checking for The Dog under the stacks of clothes, Peter thought. But now Celia had her attention. "What do you mean, Peter's lying?" she asked.

"Can't you see how guilty he looks?" Celia said. "He's got to be lying. What did you do, Peter? Did you let him run away? Why didn't you just tell Mom you didn't want a dog?"

"Peter let The Dog run away?" Izzy asked in a small voice. "Peter wouldn't do that."

Celia looked at Izzy as though she were being particularly obtuse, even for a six-year-old. "Peter's scared of The Dog. And he did something to him, I can just tell."

It was too much. For two nights now, Peter had hardly slept; he'd spent the last thirty-six hours worried and afraid. And now his sisters were staring at him, contempt visible in Celia's eyes, and Izzy...oh, the expression on Izzy's face was so much worse than anything Peter had ever seen. His baby sister was looking at him as though he just might be a monster.

And maybe he was.

"I turned him into a mushroom," Peter whispered. "That's where The Dog is. He's in a box in my closet, and he's a mushroom."

Chapter Six

Celia rolled her eyes. "You did not."

"I did too," Peter said, nettled.

"That's ridiculous."

"It's still true."

"How did you turn him into a mushroom?" asked Izzy. She appeared more confused than anything else.

"It was an accident," said Peter. "He was teaching me magic, and I lost my temper."

"Oh," said Izzy. She thought for a minute, then said, "Will you turn him back again, please? I like him."

Peter sighed. "I wish I could. I was trying all night, but I can't figure out how."

"Oh, stop it, already," said Celia. "He's not telling the truth, Izzy. You know that, right?"

"I'm not lying," said Peter. "I'll show you. The mushroom's in my closet."

"I don't know what seeing a mushroom will prove," Celia muttered, but she followed Peter and Izzy to his room anyway.

Peter closed the door behind them (in case his mother

woke up), then opened his closet. His hands were shaking as he took down the shoe box. "I put him here last night," he said. "I think he'll still be here. I mean, unless the magic wore off and he's a dog again." In which case he was probably long gone, Peter thought but didn't say: why would The Dog return to a boy whose only magical act so far had been malicious? The thought worried him enough that he held his breath as he lifted the box's lid.

But there it was, the mushroom with the plumy tail, and next to it the big white bone. The mushroom leaned sideways in its pile of dirt, and a fine dusting of soil covered its top, but as far as Peter could tell, it was still alive.

"Oh...," said Izzy.

"That's it?" asked Celia, and Peter could tell she was halfway to being convinced. Never before had a mushroom had such a, well, *canine* look to it. "That's The Dog?"

"Yes."

Peter told them the whole story, starting with dinner on the night before his birthday, when he had announced he wanted a dog when he didn't really want any such thing. He told them about seeing The Dog turn into a dragon and about sneaking off to the golf course when he was supposed to be in bed. Then he explained what The Dog had told him about magic.

"But why did you make him a mushroom?" Izzy asked.

"I shouldn't have," Peter muttered sheepishly. "I meant to wish I could fly. But he said something, and it...well, it made me mad. And before I knew it, he was a mushroom. I would've changed him back, but I couldn't make the magic work again. I really tried."

"Have you tried today?" Celia asked. "Maybe you were too tired last night. Or maybe you only get one wish a day—it works like that sometimes in books."

"I haven't tried yet this morning," Peter said. "I haven't had a chance."

"I think you should," Celia said.

So Peter tried again. He stared at the mushroom, attempting to remember exactly how his thoughts had gone last night. *Change,* he thought, as strongly as he could. *Change back into The Dog. Do it now.*

Nothing happened.

He turned to his sisters helplessly. "See?"

Celia picked up the shoe box and studied the mushroom. Peter was surprised to realize that he was glad to have Celia there. She might be kind of a pain sometimes, but she was still good in times of crisis—the best of them when there was a problem to solve, Peter's father had once said. At this moment, at least, it felt as if she was on his side.

He should have known better.

"You're a loser, Peter," Celia said, her voice matter-of-fact, as though she were commenting on the weather. "You know that, don't you? A real loser."

"Huh?"

"How dumb do you think we are?" She was building up steam now. " 'See, nothing happens,' " she whined. " 'I try and I try, but I just can't change this mushroom into a dog.' Duh, Peter. Like we were going to believe that *you* could do magic. It's easier to believe that The Dog could talk than to believe that."

Celia had often teased Peter, but never before had she sounded so deliberately cruel. That, more than her words, caused Peter's hands to curl into fists. "It's just the way my brain works," he said. "That's how The Dog explained it, anyway."

"Your brain *doesn't* work," said Celia. "Sometimes it's hard to believe you're the son of an air force captain."

Speechless, Peter stared at Celia. Then his eye fell on the shoe box where she had placed it on the carpet in front of her. The mushroom sat there in the soil, round and gray and doglike, and it made Peter angrier still, because why hadn't The Dog helped him more? Why had he taught Peter just enough to screw things up? All Peter wanted was to show Celia how wrong she was. Wrong about everything: about magic and about Peter too. *Change,* Peter thought, staring at the mushroom. He could feel the anger traveling through him, almost electric in its power. *Change into that horrible annoying dog. Come on. Do it!*

The electricity gathered, pulling together into a massive charge. And that charge had a center two inches behind Peter's right temple. *Do it,* he thought once more, and this time he knew what would happen.

There was no smoke, no rolling thunder or crackling lightning. One moment Peter was looking at a mushroom. The next he was looking at The Dog, one foot still in the shoe box, a sprinkling of dirt on his grimy white coat and a startled expression on his long face.

That taste, the taste of power, was in Peter's mouth again. He couldn't help rolling his tongue along the top of his mouth, savoring it.

"Wow!" said Izzy.

"I did it!" squealed Celia. She clapped her hands together. "I can't believe I actually did it!"

Peter turned in disbelief. "What do you mean, you did it? I was the one who changed The Dog back."

"Yes, but I was the one who figured it out," said Celia smugly.

"What are you talking about? Figured what out?"

"Ahem," said The Dog, stepping out of the shoe box. He shook his back, scattering dirt across Peter's floor. Then he held up a paw so that Celia could shake it. "Well done, Celia," he said. "I appreciate the help."

"You really can talk!" exclaimed Izzy.

"That's so cool!" said Celia. "Will you show us how you do magic?"

"Why not?" said The Dog. "I owe you, after all." He stared for a moment at the girls, and before Peter knew what was happening, his sisters were gone, replaced by two small birds. One was bright purple and one bright pink, just the colors of the feathers that a moment before had dangled in Celia's hair.

For a moment, the birds just looked at each other in astonishment. Then, while Peter watched, they began to flap around the room. They circled wildly over the bookcase, under the lamp, and around and around Peter, their delight obvious as they called back and forth to each other in shrill, happy cheeps.

The unfairness made Peter's jaw drop. "I was the one

who turned you back!" In some part of his mind, Peter knew that he shouldn't wake up his mother, but it was all he could do to keep from shouting. "Why did you make Celia into a bird? It was me! I was the one who saved you!"

The Dog made a face, and Celia and Izzy were once more standing on the floor as themselves.

"I was flying!" said Izzy.

"That was awesome!" said Celia. Her arms still hovered a few inches from her sides, as though she expected she might take off again at any moment. "Thank you, Dog!"

"Of course," said The Dog. "Now will you explain to Peter how you rescued me?"

Celia giggled. "I'd be happy to." She turned to Peter. "When I was listening to you tell your story, I was trying to figure out what was different the one time when you were able to do magic. Everything seemed the same, except that the one time when it worked, you were really mad. So I figured I'd try to make you mad again. And so I said the meanest things I could think of, and look! You were able to change The Dog back."

What she said made sense, Peter thought. He had been angry last night when he changed The Dog into a mushroom, and angry, too, today when the magic finally worked. Still...

"But why?" he demanded, looking at The Dog. "Why can I only do magic when I'm mad? And why didn't you tell me?"

The Dog scratched his ear, and his eyes shifted uneasily away from Peter's. "I wasn't sure you had to be mad," he said. "That's why I didn't tell you. There are actually a lot of different emotions that enable magicians to do magic. Greed, hate, anger—those are definitely the three big ones, but there are others, too. My old magician once made a whole house disappear because he was resentful."

Peter had about a thousand questions he wanted to ask, but before he could, Izzy spoke up. "Why did he want the house to disappear?"

The Dog snorted. "It was built closer to his house than he wanted, and it had a pool. The kids were always playing and laughing outside. He could have made it so he couldn't hear them, but instead one day, *poof!* The family that lived there thought a freak tornado had carried their home away, but then, most people will believe anything rather than believing in magic."

"So he just made their house disappear?" Celia said. The smile on her face faded.

"Yes, that's right."

"He sounds like a jerk, your magician," said Peter.

"Of course he was a jerk," said The Dog. "He was a magician."

"Can't magicians be nice?" asked Izzy.

"A magician can start out a good person," said The Dog. "I'm sure many of them are very decent kids to begin with. But from what I saw with my master, the more magic you do, the more you want to do magic. And the more you want to do magic, the more you open your mind to the bad emotions that allow you to channel your power. Sooner or later, the bad emotions become a part of who you are. Why, just look at Peter! He's still shaking with anger, and he probably can't even tell you why."

Peter looked down at his hands. He hadn't realized it before, but they were, in fact, shaking. He pressed them against his thighs.

"Are you angry, Peter?" asked Celia.

"No," Peter tried to say, but the word shot out of his mouth, sounding, well, angry.

"Why are you mad?" asked Izzy, moving closer to him.

"It's just…It's because…" Looking at Izzy, Peter couldn't actually remember why he was so angry. Celia had said mean things and taken credit for turning The Dog back into a dog. But she'd figured out how Peter's magic worked, and she had only said the mean things to help him. The Dog had turned Izzy and Celia into birds—but last night The Dog had actually taught Peter how to do magic. Wasn't that just as good as, if not better than, getting to fly? "I'm not angry anymore," he said, realizing as the words came out of his mouth that they were true. He took Izzy's hand. "I'm not sure why I was mad before. I'm sorry."

"It's not really Peter's fault," The Dog said. "It's just something that will happen if he does magic often enough. Kind of a side effect, I guess you'd call it."

"You mean if Peter does magic all the time, he's going to end up as mean as your magician?" asked Celia.

The Dog pawed the carpet. "My master met a few other magicians," he said, "and he made it sound as though they were just as evil as he was. It seems likely that will happen to Peter, too."

"But you aren't mean," said Izzy. "And you're a magician."

"Me?" said The Dog. "Magic doesn't make me angry, but I can only do it because the magician wished it. And my power is only a fraction of his."

"So Peter could be even more powerful than you?" Celia said. "He could change us into anything we want? Turn dirt into money? Do our homework? Wish us anyplace we want to go?"

"With some limits," said The Dog.

"I don't want Peter to do any more magic," Izzy said.

"But...," said Peter.

"But...," said Celia at the same time.

The Dog laughed, a snorty sort of half bark. "Once you've started doing magic, it can be hard to stop."

Izzy looked as if she were about to cry. "But I don't want him to turn mean!"

"Of course I won't do magic if you don't want me to," Peter hurriedly reassured her, the words tumbling from him at the sight of her worried face. "I promise I'm not going to become like The Dog's magician. Please don't be upset, okay?"

"But, Peter...," Celia objected.

"Izzy doesn't need to worry," said Peter. He raised his eyebrows, hoping Celia would understand.

Before Celia could respond, a door squeaked at the other end of the hallway. Celia and Peter looked at each other in alarm.

"Izzy, don't say anything to Mom about magic, or The Dog talking, okay?" whispered Celia.

"Why not?"

"She won't understand," Peter said. "And she's got

enough to worry about, with her new job and Dad being gone and all."

"All right," Izzy said, a little uncertainly.

Peter squeezed her hand, which was still in his. He would do anything to protect her, he vowed to himself. But he would find a way to save his dad at the same time, even if he had to lie to do it.

Chapter Seven

Breakfast that morning was awkward and full of long silences. Peter kept waiting for his mother to put down her cup and demand to know what was going on. But she was distracted: a frown pulled at the corners of her mouth, especially when she glanced at the newspaper half open on the counter. A story about the war, Peter guessed; probably more soldiers dead in an attack somewhere. Peter had given up reading about the war. Somehow the descriptions of battles in distant countries made his father seem farther away than ever.

Now, sitting at the breakfast table, Peter couldn't tell whether he was relieved by his mother's preoccupation or not. In a way, it would have been nice to tell her the whole story, to drop this moral dilemma on her lap and let her be the one to resolve it.

She wasn't going to make it that easy.

While Peter nibbled on his toast and scrambled eggs, his thoughts went something like this:

1. He understood how to do magic and could do it if he wanted.
2. He had promised Izzy he wouldn't do magic.
3. Doing magic might make him angry.
4. If he did magic, maybe he could bring his father home.

Four was the sticking point. In those first moments after he'd turned the mushroom back into The Dog, a small portion of Peter's mind had imagined all he could do with his newfound powers. Once The Dog had explained what happened to magicians, Peter had let go of those dreams. But his father—how could Peter not use magic to get his father back? Maybe, he argued to himself, Izzy would allow him to do one or two small spells (was that what he should call them?) if she knew what he was doing the magic for. But what if she didn't? Peter knew himself; he knew that although he wasn't extraordinarily good, he *was* ordinarily good: the sort of kid who returned lost wallets when he found them; who didn't cheat on tests or lie to his parents or accept too much change at the grocery store. Surely magic couldn't change that overnight. Maybe today Peter had been angry after he transformed The Dog back, but it had lasted for minutes only. Wouldn't being angry for a few minutes be better than risking his father's life? *Yes,* he thought. *Yes, it would.*

Celia kicked him under the table, and he realized he was nodding vehemently for no good reason.

"Mom, can I be excused?" he said.

Peter's mom glanced at his plate of half-eaten eggs. "Umm, sure. If you're really done eating."

"I think I'm going to take the dog for a walk," Peter said. "He could use some exercise."

The Dog, having finished his breakfast of kibble, was snoring in the sunlight by the kitchen window. "Okay," Peter's mother said. "Have a great walk."

"Mom, may I be excused, too?" said Celia in a rush as Peter grabbed the leash they had bought the day before. "Peter, wait for me, I'm coming," she added before her mother could answer her initial question.

"Me too," said Izzy. "I want to come, too!"

Peter clipped the leash onto The Dog's collar, then turned back to his sisters. "I thought you had a playdate this morning," he said to Izzy. "Aren't you supposed to go to Rebecca's house?"

"Oh. That's right," said Izzy, her chin sinking in disappointment.

"And aren't you going shopping with Mom?" Peter said to Celia.

"I don't need to go shopping," snapped Celia, her eyes sparking as she realized what Peter was doing.

"That's not what you said yesterday," said Peter. "I think your exact words were 'I'm going to *die* if I don't get some new sneakers!' "

Peter's mom took one last sip of coffee. "Actually, that is what you said," she reminded Celia. "And I did leave the morning open so you and I could have a shopping date."

"But . . . !" said Celia.

Peter didn't give his sister any additional time to

object. "See you in a while," he said, walking to the door with The Dog, barely awake, following. "Bye!"

"Bye, Peter," said his mom while his sisters just glared after him.

"I really needed that nap," The Dog groused as they set off down the sidewalk. Above them, the sun burned in the cloudless sky, bleaching all the color from the morning: under its unrelenting brightness, the stucco houses, the dried-up lawns, even the occasional crimson-filled flowerpots all seemed to be paler versions of their real selves. It was just after nine in the morning, and Peter guessed it was close to ninety degrees already. But the empty street meant that Peter and The Dog could talk in peace. "You're forgetting that I spent all night as a mushroom. And I've never been good at sleeping standing up," The Dog continued.

"I'm tired, too," said Peter, trying not to move his mouth. He'd had a hard enough time trying to make friends at school; he didn't need to be seen wandering down the sidewalk talking to a dog. "But there's some stuff we need to talk about, and I thought it was better to talk sooner rather than later—"

"I know, I know," The Dog interrupted. "You want me to teach you more magic, right?"

"Well," said Peter, "that's part of it. But I mostly really want to ask you a question."

The Dog's ears perked up. "Yes?"

Peter took a deep breath. "I want to know why. Why you taught me magic and went to so much trouble to get me to adopt you. None of this is by accident. You must have some sort of plan. I want to know what that plan is and how it involves me." His voice was wobbly, but he had said it; he had asked The Dog the thing that had been bothering him all morning.

"My, aren't we perceptive today," said The Dog. He stopped to sniff something in the gutter while Peter waited impatiently. "In fact, you're right," The Dog continued once he was done smelling. "There is a little favor I'd like to have you do for me."

It was what Peter was expecting. It made his heart sink in his chest nonetheless. If The Dog wanted a favor from him, it wasn't likely to be something pleasant, or The Dog would've told him already.

"So what is it?" Peter asked. "You know how to do magic—can't you do anything you want?"

"Do you remember the magician?" The Dog said. "The one who made it so I could do magic? You've never asked where he is."

"So what's the answer?" said Peter. Everything The Dog had told him so far had been so strange that he hadn't thought to wonder about the magician.

"To put it simply," said The Dog, "he's currently a rock."

If Peter hadn't just turned The Dog into a mushroom, this might have shocked him more. Still..."You mean, a rock like a stone? A piece of the earth?"

"Yes. That's what I mean."

"Why? Who changed him?"

The Dog's tail swished from side to side. "What do you mean, who?"

Peter looked at him curiously. "I mean, was it another magician?"

"Oh. Right. Not exactly. He actually changed himself. It's a pretty frequent occurrence for magicians—that, and their profound love of secrecy, are the reasons the earth isn't overrun with them. When you're doing magic, you have to concentrate; did you feel that when you did it?" Peter nodded. The Dog continued, "After magicians have been doing magic for a while, it gets harder and harder to maintain concentration. If a beginner like you forgets to concentrate, the magic just won't work. But if an experienced magician loses his concentration, the magic might go wrong. Instead of flying, he might find himself buried deep in the earth. Instead of turning a coyote into a stone, he might find himself transformed into a rock the size of a chicken."

"Is that what happened to your magician?"

"The coyote was howling one night and woke the magician up. My magician hated being woken up."

Just then, a jogger turned the corner in front of them. Peter felt almost grateful for her presence, which meant that for a moment he could pretend that none of this was happening, that he was a normal boy taking a normal walk with his normal dog. As the woman drew closer, he watched her legs pump up and down, the sweat beading on her tanned forehead. She was his mother's age, and she waved at him as she ran by. He forced himself to smile back.

He didn't say anything to The Dog until she was well past them. "So what does that have to do with me?" he asked.

"After my master learned how to do magic, he was curious to know if there were any other magicians in the world. So he set out to find some. Of the three that he found, he got into battles with two that ended with him destroying the other magicians. He didn't fight with the third, though; instead, they started talking. She's the one who told him about the inevitability of backfiring spells. That's when he got his brilliant idea. Once he knew he'd eventually self-destruct, he decided to make it so I could do magic, too. He made me his assistant so I could save him if something went wrong."

Peter stopped abruptly. "Why are you telling me this?" he asked, having already guessed the answer. There was only one answer, really, that made sense of everything that had happened over the past two days.

"My best chance at returning him to human form is you."

They stood there in silence for a minute or two before Peter's feet started moving again of their own accord, but faster now, as though by walking he could escape what The Dog had said. "There must be some mistake. How could I help you with something like that? You know how to do magic better than I do. Just wish him back."

"I've tried," said The Dog. "I'm just not powerful enough. When I couldn't turn him back myself, I used the old crystal ball trick, only for me it was a dog bowl full of water. I asked it to show me how to save the magician, and I saw your face reflected back at me. You're the answer to my problem."

"He sounds pretty horrible," said Peter.

"That's perfectly true," said The Dog. "He might well obliterate you the moment he's human again. He's destroyed magicians before."

Despite the heat, Peter shivered at the word *obliterate*. "But why would I help you, then?"

"Well," The Dog said, "it takes a lot of power to bring someone back from the other side of the world. If you get it wrong, you might end up with someone's arm or leg, but not the whole person. I'm not powerful enough to do it, and neither are you."

How had The Dog guessed? Was he reading Peter's mind even now? "So I can't bring my father home." Even saying the words out loud hurt.

"You and I may not be powerful enough," said The Dog. "But my magician is. And if you make him human again, it's possible he'll be grateful enough to help you."

Peter didn't say anything. He was thinking about his father's arm, freckled and strong and beloved. The Dog yelped once, the sound splitting the quiet of the morning. "Let me know what you decide," he said, then ran down the sidewalk. Peter let him go. Their conversation was over, and they both knew it. However it had happened, The Dog had figured out his weakness. Peter had no choice but to help The Dog with his task—and pay the price, whatever it turned out to be.

Chapter Eight

On the morning that Peter's father had been scheduled to leave, Peter had woken up with the sense that someone was in his room. He had opened his eyes to find his father sitting on the edge of his mattress, watching him.

It was early still; the light that filtered in through his blinds was gray, turning everything to shadows. Peter wanted to smile at his father, but he couldn't.

"Hey, Dad," he said instead.

"Hey, kiddo," said Peter's father. "Sorry if I woke you up."

"It's okay."

For a moment, neither of them spoke. In the silence, Peter studied his father's face. What would it be like not to see him again? Peter pushed the thought away.

"Listen," said his father, "I just wanted...Well, today is going to get busy. And I wanted a chance to say good-bye to you. Just you and me, I mean."

Peter blinked away the sudden burn of tears; his father hated to see him cry. "Okay," he mumbled.

"I'm going to miss you, kiddo. You know that, right?"

"Yeah. I know," said Peter. He couldn't bring himself to add the obvious: that he would miss his father, too. "I wish you didn't have to go," he said instead.

It was the wrong thing to say; Peter could tell by the flash of impatience on his father's face. Peter's father believed in dealing with reality; *no point in fantasizing about what's not going to happen,* he'd once told Peter. "Yeah, well, that's life," he said now, glancing down at his watch. "I guess I better get moving. Got a lot to do."

And that was when Peter got mad. Mad because whatever his father said, it *wasn't* life, it was just *Peter's* life. Mad because other kids didn't have to say good-bye to their fathers. Mad because this might be the last time he ever got to be with his dad alone. Mad because he didn't want to wake up tomorrow wondering if it would be the day his father would die.

Despite his words, Peter's father was still sitting there, waiting. What for? Peter wondered. For Peter to hug him? Tell him he loved him? Tell him good-bye?

Peter did something awful then. Something he'd remembered every day these past two months. He pulled the blankets to his chin and rolled over so he faced the wall. "I'm tired," he said in a cold voice. "I want to go back to sleep."

In the bleak light of dawn, Peter's father reached out a hand to touch Peter's shoulder; then, as if thinking better of it, he pulled it back. "Okay, kiddo," he said, and stood up and left the room.

When Peter came back to his house, he found The Dog waiting for him on the front steps.

"Let's go, then," said Peter. He was in no mood to be pleasant.

"Go where?" asked The Dog, panting. He'd clearly run all the way around the block.

"You know where. Go help your magician. The one who's going to obliterate me."

The Dog yawned. "Oh, that. We can't actually do anything until tonight. It's generally better to do everything magical in the dark, when people are less likely to notice."

Peter's mother and sisters weren't going to be home for hours, and now that Peter had decided to help The Dog, he was impatient to get started. But The Dog's expression suggested that he did not intend to discuss his decision. "What are we going to do until then?" asked Peter.

"I could use some kibble," said The Dog, licking his lips. "And then... well, then I suggest we sleep."

Yeah, right, thought Peter as he went into the house. As if he could possibly sleep when he was this worried. He fed The Dog, then went into his room and shut the door to make clear that The Dog was unwelcome. He picked up a book and began to read, but the words kept blurring on the page no matter how he struggled to focus.

He didn't know at first that he was dreaming. What he knew was that he was walking through a desert, the sand thick and yellow; not like the desert in Arizona, with its saguaros and sagebrush, but like a sandbox desert, empty and bare. The sand dragged down his feet so that he had to fight to take each step, but he was too frightened to stop walking; if he stood still, he might sink.

He was in a hurry, he realized, to get someplace, but he didn't know where.

And then he saw his father. He was standing on the top of a ridge, waving excitedly, and that was when Peter knew he was dreaming, because even asleep, he could not forget that his father was deployed. All the same, Peter tried to run forward; he took one step, then another, but the sand was getting thicker and moving was getting harder.

His father kept waving, but something about his posture changed: instead of looking eager, he looked sad. As if he were waving good-bye, Peter thought, and his eyes filled with tears. Then he looked down, and his legs had turned to rock, and he knew he would never see his father again.

Peter woke to Celia shaking his shoulder.

"Wake up, lazybones. I mean it, wake up."

"Huh?" said Peter, rubbing his eyes, which felt unaccountably wet. He couldn't quite remember what he had been dreaming or where he was.

"I said you need to wake up! It's three in the afternoon, Mom and Izzy and I have been home for ages, and Mom can't figure out why you're napping. As far as she knows, you went to bed early last night and slept in today. She's starting to wonder if you're getting sick."

"Oh." The events of the last forty-eight hours came crashing back into Peter's memory. Tonight. He had promised to help The Dog tonight.

He glanced around the room.

"The Dog isn't here," said Celia impatiently. "He's out playing fetch with Izzy. For a dog who talks and does magic, he's pretty happy to chase sticks."

Peter closed his eyes. He didn't really want to think about The Dog.

"Listen," said Celia, "in a minute, we've got to go out so Mom can see you're awake. But before we do, will you tell me what you're planning?"

"What do you mean, what I'm planning?" asked Peter, playing for time.

Celia frowned. "I mean, what's going on between you and The Dog? What did you talk about on your walk this morning?"

"We didn't talk about anything," said Peter, crossing his fingers behind his back. He hated lying, and it seemed as if he had done nothing but that these last two days. "We just took a walk, like I told you."

"Peter Lubinsky! I know you're going to do more magic, and I *know* you're going to do something to bring Dad home. You have to tell me right now! This isn't fair!"

"I promised Izzy I wouldn't do more magic," Peter reminded Celia.

"That was a lie and you know it. And now you're lying again."

"I'm not lying," lied Peter.

Celia's lips tightened into a quivering sort of grimace. She looked betrayed, Peter realized in amazement. Hurt, even. Which was strange, because Peter would have said that nothing he could do could hurt Celia. Hurt was an emotion Celia saved for when she fought with her friends, or when another girl was picked for the lead in the school play. Peter would have said she didn't care enough about him to be hurt by his actions one way or another.

He couldn't involve Celia in The Dog's task. Not with that word, *obliterate*, hanging in the air. But he couldn't exclude her, either.

"You're right," he mumbled. "I wasn't telling you the truth before. I am going to try to help Dad, it's just…It's just that I've got to do some stuff with The Dog first."

"What stuff?" asked Celia.

"I can't talk about it," said Peter miserably. "Really, I can't. I'm sorry. But I'll tell you what's going on as soon as I can, okay? And I'll tell you as soon as I figure out a way to make Dad safe, too."

Celia reached out to grab his hand. "Peter, you can't leave me out of this. I'll help you. You can't do everything all by yourself."

"I have to," said Peter. "I'm sorry, but I really do."

Celia dropped his hand abruptly. "Fine. Don't include me, then. You don't need me? Well, I don't need you, either." And with that, she disappeared down the hallway.

Peter sighed, smoothed his hair with the flat of his hand, and went out to find his mother.

That evening, things proceeded pretty much as they had the night before. Around ten o'clock, Peter announced he was going to bed. His mother kissed his cheek and told him to sleep well. Once Peter and The Dog were in his room, The Dog performed the same magic with the pillows, and then he and Peter slipped out the window and into the night. This time, though, The Dog did not take off down the sidewalk.

"So what are we doing now?" Peter whispered as they stood in his front yard.

"The rock is at the magician's house," said The Dog. "So we'll go there."

"Where does he live?" asked Peter. "Is it close by?"

"Not exactly," said The Dog. "It's about thirty miles away, at the edge of the city. Magicians like solitude."

"Umm…should I call us a taxi?" Peter asked. He tried to envision explaining to a taxi driver that he and his dog wanted to go to the middle of the desert at ten o'clock at night.

"Oh, we're not driving," said The Dog.

"How are we getting there?"

"Well," said The Dog, "I was thinking we would fly."

Magic. Of course.

"So. Let's get to it," said The Dog. "How do you suggest we approach this?"

"Approach what?"

"Making you angry, obviously. Or would you rather channel your magic through hate?"

Peter shuddered. "No. I don't hate anyone that much. Anger is fine."

"So how are we going to make you angry?" said The Dog.

"Isn't that what you do?" Peter asked.

"Look," said The Dog. "It's about time for you to start taking some responsibility for yourself. It's your magic, and it's your anger. You do it." As Peter watched, The Dog rose effortlessly into the air, then—floating about five feet above Peter's head—started to lick his tail.

Standing there in his front yard, the sky black and full of stars above him, Peter tried to focus his mind. He started by thinking about how it had felt to do magic earlier that day. He tried to summon power to that spot in his head, the same electricity that had traveled through him that morning, but nothing came. Now that he knew what to look for, he could feel that the electricity was present, that it was always present, but at the moment it was spread out around him, a soft mist that touched every inch of his skin, plus the rocks and the cactuses and the sidewalk and the house. If he wanted to do magic, he needed to pull that mist into himself. *Anger,* he thought. The Dog was right.

But how do you make yourself angry on demand? He thought of Celia, but he knew immediately that wouldn't work; he felt too guilty about the way she had avoided him all afternoon. The kids at his new school might tease him sometimes, but mostly they ignored him. How could he feel angry about that? What else did Peter have to be angry about?

Then he remembered his dream.

It returned to him in a flood: his father standing on the hill, his joyous wave slowing, turning increasingly despairing. *Good-bye,* he could see his father mouthing, although Peter was too far away to hear the words, *good-bye, kiddo, good-bye.*

In the dream, Peter had known that he would never see his father again, and that had made him incredibly sad. Now, though, he realized that another emotion had been under the sadness all along. It was unfocused and raw, but it was anger.

And with that anger came the buildup of electricity and the taste of power in Peter's mouth. He could do anything, anything at all, and no one in the world could stop him. *Fly,* he commanded the electricity, closing his eyes to focus on that spot on his head. *Fly,* he thought.

He felt his body rising, the ground no longer supporting

his feet. For a moment, he was a child being picked up by his mother. Then he opened his eyes and looked around. His feet were inches above the rocks, his head as high as the top of his bedroom window. Peter Lubinsky was flying.

Chapter Nine

"Do it like this," The Dog said, arms and legs paddling through the air. "You're not Superman, you know. The magic made you weightless, but the actual motion has to come from you."

Peter glared at him. It didn't help that he had envisioned gliding effortlessly through the sky, whereas in reality he found himself hovering helplessly a few inches off the ground. *I could turn you into mush,* he thought but didn't say.

The Dog must have seen the threat in his stare; either that, or years of dealing with a magician had taught him caution. "It's a little like swimming," he continued, in a deflated tone.

Peter, who had never liked swimming, cautiously raised his hands above his head, then brought them down again in an approximation of a breaststroke. His body pushed upward in response, almost as if he really were in water, not air. He tried again, adding a kick this time. Up he zoomed; by the time he stopped moving, he was ten feet above his house. It was easier than swimming, he thought, in the sense that small motions moved you farther. He looked down with wonder at his gray gravel roof, marked by veins of black tar. He was flying! Really flying! The anger that filled him in no way diminished his amazement that he was staring at his house from above.

"Now you're getting it," said The Dog, flying up beside him. "Next try going forward and not just up. The key is to learn to control your speed and direction at the same time."

Peter couldn't help himself: every time The Dog spoke, he wanted to smash him with the electricity that still tingled through him, sending that furry body whirling across time and space. It was such a strong impulse that it was all Peter could do to keep from acting on it. "I can figure this out by myself," he grunted instead.

The Dog sighed and obediently moved away.

For the next twenty minutes, Peter practiced his kicks and strokes and dives. It was trickier than he had initially thought: if you pushed too hard in one direction (say, toward a cactus or a chimney), it was almost impossible to stop in midair or turn around. Flying wasn't like running on the ground, where you had some traction to work with. In the air there was no resistance, so Peter had to figure out how to make corrections in his flight path by changing the way he curved his body or moved his arms.

"There, is that good enough?" Peter demanded after maybe twenty minutes of tumbling into trees and slamming into the ground. His whole body felt sore, and they still were no more than a block from his house.

"It'll do," grunted The Dog, who had been silently watching the whole time, only commenting when a car drove near or Peter got too close to a window.

"Well, let's get it over with, then," said Peter. Irritation had taken the place of his earlier dread; what could some old man stupid enough to turn himself into a rock do to someone as powerful as Peter, anyway?

The Dog gave him the strangest look; if Peter had had to describe it, he would have said it was pitying, but that didn't make sense. Not at this moment, when for perhaps the first time in his life, Peter felt not the least bit pitiable. "Whatever you say," said The Dog, taking off into the night sky, and then he was out of earshot, a streak of dirty fur racing through the stars.

From then on, no matter how fast Peter flew or how much he dawdled, that plumy tail always seemed to be exactly at the edge of his sight, no closer and no farther away than before. This suited Peter perfectly. Away from The Dog's annoying presence, Peter started to actually enjoy himself. It was like flying with his father in the Cessna, but better. Peter dove down to let his fingers skim the top of a palo verde; then swooped up, up, up, until he was shaking with cold and the air was so thin it was hard to breathe. What he liked best was the feeling of the wind wrapping itself around his body. If he moved his arms and legs correctly, he could travel amazingly fast, and the air responded by curling around him, almost as if it were racing him, or better yet, racing with him, his partner as he flew through the night.

In the blackness beneath him, swimming pools glinted like gems, and rooftops hid houses as though they were secrets. It was hard not to feel superior to all those people huddled so helplessly below. Theirs was the world of interiors, of small rooms lit by even smaller lights. Peter's was the boundless world of the night sky. He owned it all: the stars, the wind, the desert below and the planets above. He could hold out his hand, he thought, and encompass the hopes and dreams of the whole universe.

He let himself dwell on that idea for a while as he flew, following The Dog's tail. It was a satisfyingly powerful thought.

And then something strange happened. Peter was flying along, thinking how much better he was than everyone else, when out of nowhere, he heard Izzy's voice asking him for a glass of water. Logically, Peter knew this couldn't be real. Still, her voice was so clear that when Peter heard it, he turned his head to answer and was surprised to find only empty sky. *Izzy isn't here,* he reminded himself, and then tried to return his mind to the subject of his own superiority. But it was a little like waking up from a dream that makes perfect sense one moment and none at all the next. You can't just shut your eyes and go back into a vision that daylight has revealed to be ridiculous. How could he be superior to Izzy? That couldn't be right.... And then one thing after another stopped being right: first his sense of being better than everyone; then his anger at The Dog; then his own fearlessness, which now struck him as laughable.

Below him, the houses had grown fewer and fewer as they flew deeper into the desert. At the same time, the darkness had grown larger, seeping like spilled ink into every corner of the earth and sky. Above him, the crescent moon seemed to smile mockingly. It was all so empty, Peter thought. How could he have failed to notice that before? How could he not have realized how lonely flying was, up here so far above the rest of the world?

With a kind of relief, he saw that in front of him, The Dog had finally slowed down and was in effect treading water in midair.

The Dog raised his nose as Peter came near, as if he were sniffing him.

"Hey," said Peter when he got close enough that The Dog could hear him.

The Dog laughed his snorty laugh. "Feeling better, are you?"

"I don't know about better.... More like myself, anyway."

"How long did it last?"

Peter didn't need to ask what *it* was. "Until a few minutes ago."

"Longer this time, huh?"

Peter just shrugged in answer. What could he say? The strangest part, the thing that he was too embarrassed to tell The Dog, was that he could still feel that person, the angry one who was both him and not him, inside his mind, pushing to get out. Peter shivered at the thought.

"So that's the magician's house," said The Dog, pointing downward with his nose.

They had reached the outer rim of lights. This was the spot where human habitation ended; beyond was the endless dark of the empty desert, interrupted only by jutting fists of even blacker rock. The houses out here were all expensive, and most were enormous complexes centered on two or three or four acres of land. From where Peter hovered, he could see the curved tiles of some roofs, the flat silver surfaces of others.

And then there was the magician's house.

It was less house than palace. As Peter and The Dog dropped down to the path that led to the entrance, Peter could feel all his earlier fear returning. What sort of power would it take to build a house like this? The front door alone was easily three times Peter's height and made entirely of copper. On either side of the door stood massive pillars, and next to the pillars were matching spiral staircases that led to a gigantic balcony above. There were windows everywhere, as tall as the door, but nothing was visible behind them: they were windows that were meant to be looked out of, not into.

"So what do you think of my old home?" asked The Dog, his lip curling in an expression Peter couldn't read.

"Umm...it's big," said Peter.

"Wait until you see it on the inside," said The Dog. "It's bigger in there than out here. I mean, he didn't want to be ostentatious or anything."

"Oh."

"He liked to sit on the balcony," The Dog continued. "You'll find that one of the biggest problems magicians face is boredom. Once you can do or have anything you want, nothing is all that interesting. So my magician made it so he could hear and see whatever he wanted, and then he spent his evenings eavesdropping on the neighbors. He'd look around until he found something interesting and tune in as if it were his own personal television program. If the show got boring, he could always force one of the 'characters' to say or do something they hadn't intended. Make them quit their jobs or fight with their families. Anything to keep it dramatic. Lots of divorces in this neighborhood after we moved in."

"He messed up people's lives?"

"Oh, yes. Many times. He thought it was funny."

Peter looked again at the house: with all those dark windows, it reminded him of a dragon who was pretending to sleep but who was really watching you. "Wouldn't I be better off trying to become more powerful on my own?" he asked. "So I could bring my dad back myself?"

"Maybe," said The Dog. "But to become more powerful, you'll have to get angrier. By the time you're powerful enough, you may be too angry to want him back anymore."

Peter shivered. "What makes you think the magician will help me?"

"I don't know if he'll help you," said The Dog. "I never know what he's going to do. One day last spring he woke up in a good mood, and we played fetch for hours. Another day he came home in a fury—I don't know why—and took away my name."

"What do you mean, he took away your name?"

"There's not much you can take away from a dog; we're pretty simple creatures. But names—they're important to us. So that's what he took. Now I don't even remember what it used to be, and it doesn't work when I try to give myself a new one."

"Why do you want to turn him back, then?" asked Peter. "Isn't it better that he's a rock?"

"It's complicated," said The Dog.

"But you must hate him," Peter said.

The Dog was silent for a long moment. Then, almost inaudibly, he said, "No, I don't hate him."

"Why not?"

"Because I knew him before."

"Before? Oh... before." Before he became a magician, Peter realized. Before he built this monstrous house; before he destroyed marriages out of boredom; before he stole The Dog's name. "He was nice before?"

The Dog was quiet for a minute, his gaze still on the massive front door. "He was terrific," he finally said, then stood up and padded on silent paws toward the house. Peter followed, his feet crunching on the rocky path. He half hoped they wouldn't be able to get in, but the door swung open the moment The Dog touched it with his nose. Without a backward glance, The Dog slipped inside, disappearing immediately into darkness.

Peter hesitated one last time, then stepped into the magician's house.

Chapter Ten

Peter was standing in the middle of what looked like an enormous carnival, with games and rides and booths stretching out in all directions as far as his eye could see. "Whac-a-Mole, Whac-a-Mole, Whac-a-Mole!" cried a man to Peter's left, waving a mallet in Peter's general direction but not really looking at him. "Popcorn, get your free popcorn!" shouted a woman to his right, robotically shaking a bag of popcorn so that it fell like snow to the ground. "It's the fastest drop in the universe!" declared another man, gesturing toward a ride that seemed to reach impossibly high into the sky. "It's the fastest drop in the universe!" the man repeated a moment later, in exactly the same tone.

Peter didn't know what he had expected, but certainly not this. There was no roof. There were no walls. And aside from the vendors working the booths and rides, there were no people, either. It was like nothing he had ever seen: at once tantalizing—the sounds, the smells, the promise of fun!—and disturbing, because it felt so, well, *wrong*.

From wherever he must have been hiding in the shadows, The Dog materialized at Peter's side.

"So what do you think of it?" The Dog asked, ignoring the vendors, who continued to recite their spiels without regard for whether anyone was actually listening.

"Where are we?" asked Peter.

The Dog chuckled. "The magician's house, of course."

"It doesn't feel like a house."

"What were you expecting?" The Dog asked. "A living room with a sofa and a TV? The magician has one of those, too, hidden around here someplace, but it certainly wouldn't make for an impressive entry."

"Is it real?" asked Peter. "The games, I mean, and the rides and food, too? What about the people? They don't seem like illusions."

"Oh, it's all real enough," said The Dog. "It's easy to change one thing into another; you know that. Creating life, now, that's a lot trickier. My magician solved that problem by transforming one living thing into another. For example, all the people who work here were once plants. That guy over there," he said, pointing with a paw to the Whac-a-Mole man, "used to be a ficus. Still is in his heart. You'll find that the people in this house don't have much going on upstairs. You can make a ficus into a man, but at his core, he still knows he's a plant. Just the way I was still me even when I was a mushroom."

Peter looked more closely at the Whac-a-Mole man. Now that The Dog had told him, he could see the greenish tinge to the man's skin. The man even waved the mallet as if it were a branch bowed by the wind.

Peter smiled tentatively, but the ficus man didn't smile back.

"The magician didn't program this lot to do much," The Dog continued, "just say their lines over and over again. They could have been more sophisticated, but the magician didn't often use this room. He saw a carnival one morning, thought he wanted one, and over the next few days, built this. When he was finished, he spent a few hours whacking the moles and riding the rides, and then he was done. But he left it here because it made for a grand entrance."

"Do the plants *mind*?" asked Peter.

The Dog scratched his car. "It's hard to know," he said. "As I told you, they're not all that bright. Would they rather be sitting in a pot of soil? Undoubtedly. Do they spend their days dwelling on the unfairness of the universe? Probably not."

Peter looked once more at the ficus man. His leaf-shaped eyes looked sad, no matter what The Dog said. Peter's sense of the wrongness of all this was getting worse, not better. "How do we get out of here?" he asked. There was nothing like a door anywhere in sight.

"Don't you want to whack a mole?" said The Dog.

Peter shuddered. "No. I just want to go."

"Right this way, then," said The Dog, and took off, weaving through the booths. Peter stumbled behind him. All around them, the plant people continued to call enticements, until Peter finally put his hands over his ears to shut out the noise.

The Dog stopped in front of a haunted house ride. A series of open cars rolled by on the track, then disappeared into a dark tunnel. "Two tickets," The Dog said to the man at the gate.

"Get your chills and thrills here!" the man said, sticking the tickets in The Dog's mouth, and then—in what struck Peter as a waste of time—taking the tickets back and opening the gate.

"Thanks," said Peter as he walked through. The man, he noticed, had whisker-like needles coming out of his ears.

"Get your chills and thrills here!" the man responded.

"Cactus?" Peter whispered to The Dog.

"Cactus," The Dog confirmed.

They climbed into the next car that came by. Hoping they weren't really about to enter a haunted house, Peter snapped the seat belt over his lap. As the car moved into the tunnel, the noise of the carnival faded away. The inside of the ride was so dark that Peter could see nothing, and panic welled up in him: what if he were stuck in this darkness forever? The third time he blinked, though, he knew even before he opened his eyes that everything had changed. The silence itself was different; it was warmer, the silence of things waiting, not the silence of emptiness.

Peter was in a restaurant. No, it was a kitchen, but it felt like a restaurant. The floor was covered with red-and-white-checked tiles; the walls were painted a cool lime green; and the kitchen counters were spotless stainless steel. A man was chopping onions next to the stove; he wore a tall chef's hat and a white apron, and he didn't seem to have noticed Peter and The Dog sitting at the kitchen table. Because they were now sitting at the kitchen table, Peter realized with a start: the haunted house car had disappeared, although Peter's hands still curled around the empty air where the seat belt had been. Across from him, The Dog perched on a red stool, his gaze focused on a menu that lay open on the table.

A teenage boy wearing wire-rimmed glasses and carrying a notepad scurried across the room from where he had been waiting in a corner. When he reached the table, he cleared his throat.

"Can I take your order?" he asked, his voice unexpectedly high-pitched. Unlike the carnival people, he actually looked at Peter and The Dog when he spoke, although his gaze was quick and nervous, as if he were expecting one of them to pounce.

"Are you ready?" The Dog asked Peter.

"Ready for what?" asked Peter.

"Ready to order, of course. You can read the menu, but if nothing on it sounds good, the chef can make pretty much anything you like."

"How did...," Peter started to say, and then stopped himself. When it came to magic, there was no point in asking how. "Does the car always stop in the kitchen?" he said instead.

"It will take you to any room in the house," The Dog said. "Depends on what's in your head when you go through the tunnel."

"Is the magician here, then?" Peter didn't see a rock.

The Dog looked slightly abashed. "Actually, he's not. I meant to be thinking of his bedroom, but I must have gotten a little distracted." His stomach growled. "The chef here makes steak and onions just the way I like them."

"We're here because you're hungry?"

The Dog shrugged.

"We're supposed to be finding the magician so he can obliterate me. And now we're stopping for a kibble break?"

"Kibble?" The Dog said, insulted. "For steak and onions. Don't get me wrong; I've enjoyed my stay with your family. But the dog food diet is really getting to me. And although magic food tastes good, it's just not as satisfying as the real thing."

It started as a burning in the center of Peter's chest, then spread outward, until it felt as if his whole body were in flames. Only, it wasn't fire; it was anger burning through him. In the little part of Peter's brain that remained Peter, a voice said there was something wrong with this reaction. What did it matter if The Dog wanted to eat? That voice was tiny, though, and easily overwhelmed by the fury that had taken over Peter's body. He was so angry he couldn't speak, just sat there fuming at the high-handed audacity of The Dog, who was wasting Peter's time to have a snack.

But I didn't perform any magic! the little voice that was Normal Peter complained in bewilderment. *I shouldn't feel like this!*

Angry Peter didn't bother to respond.

The Dog didn't seem to notice Peter's reaction. "The usual," he told the waiter. "And a big bowl of water."

The teenager turned toward Peter, peering at him through his glasses. "I don't want anything," Peter snapped.

The waiter retreated, jotting the words down on his

pad, and the chef, behind him, started a whirl of motion, onions flying, knives flickering, the sizzle of grilling meat filling the air. It smelled delicious, and Peter found himself suddenly starving; nonetheless, he sat with his arms crossed on his chest and glowered at his dining companion. His hunger made him more furious; even his own body was turning against him.

It was maybe three minutes before the waiter scurried back with The Dog's food. As Peter watched, The Dog lapped up most of his bowl of water, then began methodically working his way through his steak.

Peter sat silent for as long as he could stand it. It wasn't very long. "Are we going to get on with this soon?" he asked when The Dog was about half finished.

The Dog glanced up at a clock Peter hadn't noticed before. It was already after one AM, which meant they had left Peter's house more than three hours earlier. "Soon enough," The Dog grunted, steak juice dripping down his beard.

What bothered Peter most, he realized, was The Dog's assumption that he was in charge.

"I want to go now," said Peter, standing up and pushing back his chair.

The Dog didn't bother to look up from his plate. "I'm not done yet."

Peter leaned over and shoved The Dog's plate to the floor. It fell on the tiles with a clatter, steak and onions splattering across the spotless red and white. "Now you are," Peter said.

The Dog growled. Really growled, a loud, low sound that echoed through the kitchen, so that even the oblivious cook paused for a moment in his seemingly endless chopping. "Waiter!" The Dog called through bared teeth. "I'd like another steak. Make it well done, and take your time."

Someplace inside, Normal Peter trembled. "I'm going," said Angry Peter.

"Good luck finding the magician," retorted The Dog.

"No problem," said Peter, his eyes already scanning the room. This new self always seemed to have a plan. "You," he said to the cowering waiter. "You must know where to find the magician."

The waiter backed farther into his corner. "Yes."

"Take me there," demanded Peter. "Now."

The waiter cast a frightened look at The Dog, who responded by turning back to his bowl of water. "Umm . . . this way," the waiter said to Peter, and scurried toward one of the doors.

Chapter Eleven

Without a backward glance, Peter followed the waiter out of the kitchen. Now, he thought, they would finally get somewhere. He didn't know what he expected to see on the other side of the door: the carnival again, perhaps, or maybe the magician's bedroom, although that seemed too easy. Something *exciting*, that was the only thing he was sure of. Instead, he found himself in a long, ordinary-looking hallway. It had brown carpet on the floor and beige paint on the walls, and every few feet stood another closed door, just like the one that had swung shut behind him. It reminded Peter of his pediatrician's office building. It must be the servants' corridor, he realized; after all, the servants would need some way to get from one room to another.

While Peter took stock of the new situation, the waiter hurried ahead, moving surprisingly fast for someone who had once been a plant. By the time Peter started to follow, the waiter was maybe a hundred feet down the hallway and showed no signs of slowing.

"You!" Peter demanded. "Stop there. Wait for me."

The waiter stood quivering until Peter caught up. "Yes, sir?" he asked. His dark eyes darted from floor to door to wall to ceiling, but never to Peter.

The idea of servants was appealing in the abstract. In reality, Peter couldn't figure out quite how to address a trembling boy who looked perhaps five years older than he was. "I want to know what sort of plant you are," he demanded.

The boy's eyes darted more rapidly than ever. "I'm not a plant."

"Oh." Peter thought for a moment. "Then what are you?"

"I'm... I'm a mouse, sir."

"A mouse." This made perfect sense but sent a shiver of revulsion climbing Peter's spine. A mouse forced to be a human. There was something wrong with that, wasn't there? But no, why would that be wrong? The mouse probably liked being a human. He also probably liked getting to work for a powerful magician, a magician like Peter.

"Well, keep going," said Peter. "We haven't got all night. But walk more slowly this time, so I can keep up."

"Yes, sir." The mouse-waiter scurried forward again, looking just as fearful as before but moving less quickly.

Peter, following, rapidly became lost in thought. For the first time, he started to wonder what would happen to this house and its inhabitants if he wasn't able to change the magician back. Who knew what astonishing things hid behind each of these doors? Perhaps if Peter failed in his task, the house would eventually revert to its original state, just as the illusion of Peter and The

Dog had disappeared in the morning light. The carnival would crumble; these doors would disappear; the waiter would once more be a mouse. The magician must have put years of work into creating something this magnificent. And soon it might be gone.

Peter thought of his own house, identical to all the others on his block, with white paint that didn't fully disguise the dings and nail holes left by other people's pictures. In all of their moves from base to base, his family had never had a house that was truly *theirs*.

Magic could change all that. Peter could wish his mother a library and his father a gym. Celia might like a roller rink, and as for Izzy, Peter would build her a butterfly garden, filling it with flowers and fluttering wings. For himself, Peter would create a rocket room, with windows that showed the stars and planets the way they actually looked from space. It would be easy enough to do; there was, after all, that electricity hovering around him, just waiting to be used, wanting to be used....

Would it be so bad, he wondered, if he thought himself a Snickers bar? He was just focusing his anger to do magic when his clumsiness saved him. One of his feet somehow ended up in front of the other, sending him sprawling onto the carpet. The fall knocked the breath out of him, and the shock of it knocked something else out of him as well. As he lay there on the carpet, trying to breathe, he realized he had stopped feeling so angry; in fact, he felt pretty much like the old Peter, though he could sense that Angry Peter was still there under the surface.

From his new vantage point, he could see the red

high-top sneakers of the trembling waiter, shifting uneasily as if he wanted nothing more than to be off. Looking at those sneakers, Peter realized that he had been following the waiter for a long time. A really long time. He lifted his head, but he still couldn't see an end to the hallway. What sort of magician created a house where it would take hours for his servants to reach him?

Peter sat up but didn't get to his feet. "Could you please tell me what's behind all these doors?" he asked the mouse-waiter.

The mouse-waiter looked confused by the change in Peter's tone. "Oh, I wouldn't know that."

"So which door will we go through?"

The mouse-waiter tilted his head sideways. Peter could almost see quivering whiskers. "Umm... the open one?"

"Which open one?" asked Peter.

"There's only ever one open one."

"And that's to the magician's bedroom?"

"That's to wherever the magician is. How else could we find him?"

The mouse-waiter's roundabout logic was beginning to make a certain amount of sense. "So you walk until you see an open door, and then you go through, and that's how you find the magician?" Peter asked.

"Yes. Of course."

"When was the last time you saw the magician?"

The mouse-waiter's dark eyes went wide with fright. "It was the last time I saw him!" he said. "The last time I saw him was the last time I saw him!"

The Dog had played a trick on him, Peter saw at once. He had let Peter leave with the mouse-waiter, knowing full well that the mouse-waiter couldn't find the magician until the magician opened a door, which the magician—being a rock—couldn't do. And if Peter hadn't tripped... Well, Peter might have ended up walking down this hallway forever, adrift in daydreams and angry thoughts.

Peter stood up, brushing off his pants, and when the mouse-waiter started once more down the hallway, he didn't follow. Instead he reached out his hand, grabbed the nearest knob, and twisted.

He half expected it to be locked—in fact, that was probably why he was brave enough to try it in the first place. But the knob turned, and the door swung open.

And that was when the most magical thing of all happened.

Behind the door was a room. But it wasn't just any room: it was Peter's bedroom at home, with his piles of moving boxes and his homework half done where he had left it on his desk. There was the model F-117 Nighthawk he'd made with his dad when he was seven. The chessboard he'd gotten for his birthday last year. The fish tank that had been empty since they'd moved.

There wasn't anything beautiful about the scene in front of him: it was just the slightly messy bedroom of a now-twelve-year-old boy. But seeing it made Peter's heart light. His mind whirled, trying to put what he knew or thought he knew together in a way that made sense. This was what became clear:

1. His room could not be in the magician's house.
2. Peter could therefore not be in the magician's house.

It followed logically that all of this, these crazy events that had seemed so incredible and unlikely, must in fact *be* incredible and unlikely. Peter had wondered if it was a dream, he remembered, when The Dog had first started talking. And standing in his room, Peter knew he had been right then, and that he was just now waking up to find himself once more at home.

As his certainty grew, he could feel an involuntary smile spread across his face. On the other side of his walls, he thought, Celia, Izzy, and his mother must be at this moment sleeping in their beds. Tomorrow morning he would wake up and eat pancakes with his family; everything would make sense once more. For now, he found his favorite pajamas in his drawer, changed out of his clothes, and crawled between his flannel solar system sheets. His bed had never felt so comfortable and welcoming in his life.

Chapter Twelve

He woke to the sound of dog laughter.

"No," Peter said, his eyes still closed. "You're a dream. Go away. I don't want to dream you anymore."

The snorty laughter continued, a soft, genuinely amused sound. "Is that what you're telling yourself now?" asked The Dog.

"That's what I know," said Peter. "I refuse to believe in you. I'm not going to talk to you anymore, because you're not even here."

The laughter died away, and the room fell silent. Peter, warm between his sheets, thought after a minute that perhaps his words had worked; that all he needed to banish his dream was the sheer willpower to tell The Dog to go. He was just starting to settle back to sleep when The Dog said, "I find it pretty funny that you're in this room."

"There's nothing funny about it," said Peter, who hadn't meant to answer. "It's my room. Where else should I be?"

"It's not actually your room," said The Dog. "You know you're still in the magician's house, right?"

"I can't be in the magician's house," said Peter, stubbornly unwilling to open his eyes to talk to someone who he knew was just in his head. "Why would the magician build my room in his house? It's nothing special, just my room. The fact that I found it here means you're not real and this is just a dream. I won't let you convince me otherwise."

"Whatever you say," said The Dog, and yawned. "If I'm not real, then I might as well take a nap."

"Fine," snapped Peter.

"Fine," said The Dog, and the room got quiet again.

It wasn't the same quiet as before, though. Try as he might, Peter couldn't recapture his previous sense of peace. The thing was, it didn't make sense. Dreams didn't come to pester you and try to wake you up. They didn't argue with you. They certainly didn't take naps. The wise thing to do, Peter thought, would be to see if his sisters and mother were sleeping in their rooms; if they were, he would know that his bedroom was real. Sighing, he opened his eyes, then pushed back his blankets stealthily, hoping The Dog wouldn't notice.

"Where are you going?"

"To the bathroom," Peter lied.

"Peter, this is all very sweet," said The Dog, getting up from where he'd been sitting on the carpet next to Peter's bed, "but it's getting close to dawn, and I'm going to need your help with the magician soon."

"I don't understand," said Peter. "What's sweet?"

"This," said The Dog, gesturing around the room with his nose. "It's not your room. Shall I show you?"

The Dog closed his eyes. He made a face as if he were pooping. And Peter found himself sitting on the cold, rough floor of what appeared to be a room-sized concrete box.

And he was naked.

Shivering, Peter scrambled toward his clothes, which were piled in the corner where a few moments before his laundry hamper had been. As soon as he had pulled on his jeans, he turned to The Dog accusingly. "What did you do to my room? Why do you keep doing these things to me? Why can't you just leave me alone?"

The Dog looked surprisingly regretful. "I wish I could. But your room was never here, you know. You were always lying on the concrete. Do you remember when you asked me if the carnival was real or an illusion? Well, the carnival was real, but your room was an illusion, a very fancy illusion."

"Why would the magician create an illusion of my room?"

"He didn't. Or didn't exactly. The spell creates an illusion of whatever a person most desires. Some kids walking in would find themselves suddenly movie stars; others might discover an arcade filled floor to ceiling with video games or other toys."

Peter tried to imagine the enormous power it would take to create a spell like that. Changing a plant into a person was one thing, but how could someone create an illusion that changed depending on who walked through a door? "That doesn't make any sense," he argued. "I didn't find any of that stuff. I just found my room."

"I know. That's what I thought was funny. You could have been anywhere—but the place you most wanted to be was your own house."

Now that Peter understood, he knew why The Dog had been laughing at him, and it angered him to realize how his innermost self had been exposed for The Dog's amusement. The anger in turn brought a bit of that other Peter, the mean one. Peter could feel it in the way his back suddenly straightened.

"You've had your laugh," he said, shrugging on his T-shirt. "Now let's get on with the magician. As you said, it's close to dawn." He stalked toward the door.

"Wait," said The Dog. "There's something I wanted to ask you."

"What?" Peter couldn't help sounding angry. He *was* angry.

"Do you remember when we were flying? And you were so mad?"

"Yes...," said Peter, confused by the change in subject.

"Did something in particular snap you out of it? The anger, I mean? Or did it just gradually wear off?"

Peter remembered the moment perfectly. "It was Izzy. I heard her voice asking me for a drink of water. Which didn't make any sense, because she was miles away, but that was when I started feeling more...well, more like me." Even talking about Izzy now made him feel less angry, Peter realized.

"I wonder...," murmured The Dog. "It's possible, I suppose."

"What's possible?"

"I'm going to do it," The Dog said. "It's worth the risk."

"What risk? What are you going to do?"

Instead of answering, The Dog closed his eyes and made that face again. Some part of Peter must have sensed what was coming; the moment he realized that The Dog was performing magic, he leapt toward The Dog's back, as if flattening him might stop him. But it was too late.

As he landed on The Dog, both of them collapsing onto the concrete, Peter saw that sleeping on the floor in front of him was Izzy, her hands cradling her head as if she were grasping a pillow. And behind him...

"Finally!" said a familiar voice.

Peter turned. There was Celia, wearing her nightshirt, with a book in one hand and a stick in the other.

"You brought my sisters?"

From under him, The Dog said, "Will you... *mmph...* get off me, you oaf?"

"I can't believe you brought my sisters!" yelled Peter, not budging. "You have to send them back!"

Izzy woke up. "Peter!" she said, smiling. Her smile faltered, though, as she noticed her unfamiliar surroundings. "Where are we?"

"Oh, no," groaned Peter, not moving off The Dog. "Please send them back. Please. You don't know what you've done."

"I can't send them back," said The Dog smugly.

"What do you mean, you can't?"

"I mean I can't. I've done too much magic today. I told you that transporting people takes a lot of power. I can only do it for short distances, and it uses pretty much every bit of power I have. If I tried to send them back right now, it wouldn't be safe."

Peter buried his face in his hands.

"So you might as well get off me," The Dog added.

"Besides," said Celia, "I don't want to go back. Not until I know where I am, anyway."

"What's going on?" asked Izzy. "I don't think I like this place."

"I can't breathe," said The Dog. "I'm going to have to bite you if you don't move."

Peter moved. He didn't get off the floor, though. He felt weighed down by despair.

"Obviously you don't want us here," said Celia, "but would you tell us what this place is anyway?"

"Yes, please," said Izzy, looking a little more awake. Creeping closer to The Dog, she entwined her small fingers in the fur at the back of his neck. The Dog didn't seem to mind. In fact, after a moment, he slumped over so his head was in her lap.

"We're in the house where The Dog's master lives," said Peter, trying to think how to quickly summarize the events of the last few hours. "He accidentally turned himself into a rock, and The Dog wants to change him back. The reason The Dog taught me magic is that he needs my help."

Celia grinned. "Sounds exciting."

"It might be exciting," said Peter, "except for the fact that there's a good chance the magician will kill us if I manage to make him human."

"Oh," said Celia.

Izzy's hand on The Dog's neck froze. "You promised you wouldn't do more magic."

And there it was: the moment Peter had most been dreading, the real reason, he realized, that he had felt so sick when The Dog had brought his sisters to the magician's house. There was no hiding the truth. "I lied to you," he said, more roughly than he intended. "I've done magic more than once already, and I'm going to do it again. And it *is* changing me—making me angrier and meaner, and not just when I'm doing the magic, but all the time."

"But you knew that was going to happen," said Celia. "That's what The Dog told you. But you decided to do it anyway so that you could bring Dad home, right?"

"Is that why you did magic?" asked Izzy. "For Daddy?"

"The Dog says I'm not powerful enough to bring Dad back myself," Peter said. "But he thinks the magician might help us if I make him human again. Or he might kill us; The Dog doesn't know. I thought it was worth the chance."

For a minute, Izzy sat silently. Then she put her face down low, so her nose was right against The Dog's. "Isn't there another way Peter could do magic? So he doesn't have to be mean?"

The Dog gave a barking laugh. "I really, truly wish I knew how."

"Oh, Izzy," said Celia. "You're too little to understand. Peter has to protect Dad if he can."

Peter felt a wave of gratitude toward Celia.

Izzy looked unhappy, but after a moment she nodded.

"Great! Now that that's settled," said Celia, blowing her bangs out of her eyes, "let's get going! I want to see more of the house."

"It's about time," said The Dog. He gave a shake and stood up with great dignity, as though he had not spent the last five minutes being petted by a six-year-old. He walked to the door with Izzy and Celia following.

Peter came last. He should be happy, he thought: he had gotten Izzy to agree to let him do magic. That was what he wanted, right? But he didn't feel happy. They were still in the magician's house, after all, and their father wasn't even close to being home safely.

When they exited the concrete box that had been Peter's room, they found themselves in the long hallway once again. The Dog trotted in front, leading the way, with Celia following eagerly. Peter trailed behind, and after a minute Izzy did, too, slipping back to walk next to him. Peter wanted to grab her hand, but he couldn't quite bring himself to do it. They walked in silence, all four of them, down the empty hallway; each step Peter took required an effort of will.

And then, just as the quiet became more than Peter could bear, he noticed something and burst out laughing.

Izzy, Celia, and The Dog stopped immediately.

"What is it?" asked The Dog. "Is something wrong?"

Peter tried to answer, but he couldn't squeeze words past the laughter bubbling up in his chest.

"Are you okay, Peter?" asked Celia.

It was hopeless. "You're...you're holding *Harry Potter*!"

Celia glanced down as if noticing the book in her hands for the first time. A flush climbed her cheeks.

"And...and a stick," he choked out.

"I don't understand," said Izzy. "What's so funny?"

Celia stood there, blushing and watching Peter laugh. Then slowly her shoulders started to shake. The corners of her mouth twisted up. And she, too, was laughing, laughing as uncontrollably as Peter. Her laughter set Peter off again, and his did the same to her, so that for several minutes neither of them could stop.

"Why are you laughing, guys?" Izzy demanded.

"Well," said Peter, wiping his eyes, "I *think* the funny part is that when The Dog brought Celia here, she was trying to learn to do magic by reading *Harry Potter* and pretending a stick was a wand."

"I wasn't pretending the stick was a wand!" protested Celia. "I was using it to poke myself in the head. To try to find the right spot."

This made Peter laugh so hard he almost fell down. "But why would you want to learn to do magic anyway?" he asked when he could speak again. "And what made you think *Harry Potter* would help?"

"I figured anyone who wrote so much about magic probably knew about real magicians," Celia said, "and I still think I'm right. I bet there's more hidden in this book than we know. And I wanted to learn to do magic because you were leaving me out, and I was pretty sure you'd need me sooner or later. I know you don't like me, but I told you: I'm a part of this. The Dog knows it, too;

that's why you brought us here, right?" she asked, turning to The Dog.

"Something like that," said The Dog. "Although I have to tell you: I doubt if you could learn to do magic."

"I'm good at using my brain," said Celia, bristling.

"No," said The Dog, "I didn't mean the problem was you. But most people aren't able to do magic, you know. When my master went looking for other magicians, he only found five in the whole world. Seems unlikely that one family would have two potential magicians in it. What are the odds?"

"Oh," said Celia. Her lips turned down in disappointment.

Peter was still absorbing what Celia had said. "I like you," he said. "You're the one who doesn't like me. Because I embarrass you."

Celia rolled her eyes. "You and Izzy leave me out all the time. You only include me when you have to. Like now."

"That's not true," said Peter, but even as he said it, he realized she was right. "Besides, you always have so many friends and stuff."

"I still don't like to be left out," Celia said. "That's just mean."

No one had ever called Peter mean before, and he had never imagined that was how Celia saw his actions. "I'm glad you're here now," he said. "Really."

"Now that we've got that out of the way, do you think we could get going again?" asked The Dog. If he'd had a wristwatch, thought Peter, he would have been frowning at it and tapping his paw on the carpet.

They started down the hallway once more, but the mood was different than it had been before. Now the children walked side by side, occasionally giggling when someone bumped into someone else. Once Peter found himself squeezing Celia's hand, almost as if she were Izzy. He dropped it quickly, but not before Celia smiled.

The Dog stopped in front of one of the doors.

"This is it?" asked Celia.

"This is it," said The Dog. He touched his nose to the door: it swung open immediately. Only darkness was visible beyond the doorway, darkness that swallowed The Dog piece by piece, nose to tail, as he stepped through. Peter took a deep breath. It was really going to happen. He was going to confront the magician.

"Izzy and Celia, I think you should wait in the hallway," he said, trying to sound appropriately big-brotherish. "I'll just be a minute."

"Really?" said Celia. "Okay. If you think that's best."

Peter's shoulders sagged in relief. He couldn't believe it had been that easy.

Then Celia smiled, a slightly wicked smile that Peter knew all too well, and she disappeared through the doorway after The Dog. "Celia!" Peter shouted, but it was too late.

Izzy turned to Peter. "I don't want to wait all by myself."

Peter didn't want to take Izzy with him, but he didn't want to leave her alone in the magician's house, either. He grasped her hand, and they stepped into the blackness together.

Chapter Thirteen

One moment they were in the hallway, the next they were standing next to Celia, whose mouth had dropped open in surprise. Peter, too, stared at the room in astonishment. "Holy cow," he said under his breath.

Izzy edged closer to him. "What are all these monster bones?" she whispered.

"They're not monster bones," said Peter. He blinked, unable to fully believe what he was seeing. "They're dinosaur fossils."

"It's like a museum," breathed Celia. "Only not at all boring."

No museum in the world had this many fossils, Peter thought; and no museum felt so, well, *alive.* Vines hung from the ceiling, thick-leafed and glossy; trees grew from the dirt floor, their branches curving and twining like prehistoric snakes. Unlike the carnival, which had had no ceiling or walls, this was distinctly a room, but a room like none Peter had seen before. It was as big as a stadium, he thought: it had to be, because how else could it hold so many dinosaurs?

The dinosaurs stretched beneath trees. They peered out from bushes. They hung frozen in the air, paralyzed in midflight. Everywhere Peter looked, dinosaur bones stood as though the flesh had just dropped from them, leaving behind only the whitened skeletons of the great and terrifying beasts. Peter remembered his dreams of a rocket bedroom. That was nothing compared to the magnificence of this place.

"There must be a thousand dinosaurs in here," he whispered. There was something weighty about the silence that made it hard to speak in a normal voice. "Do you see that? The tall one? It's an Allosaurus. That's a Coelophysis over there—the little guy. That's a Pteranodon...not strictly a dinosaur, but close enough. Those look like Microraptors, maybe?"

"That one's definitely a Velociraptor," said Celia, pointing to her left. "We learned about those last week in school."

"What's the one behind the bed?" asked Izzy.

Peter had been deliberately avoiding looking at the bed, which stood directly in front of them, positioned as if the room's owner wanted to watch the door even in his sleep. Now Peter glanced at the bony figure towering above it. One foot was planted on either side of the headboard, as if the dinosaur were guarding what slept beneath. "See how it has only two fingers?" said Peter. "That means it's a Tyrannosaurus rex. The king of the terrible lizards."

The Dog nodded. "The dinosaurs were the magician's big project," he explained. "He used magic to pull fossils from the earth, piece by fragmented piece.

Each of these dinosaurs took days of his time, which is a lot for a magician. I think the intensity with which he worked on them is probably what allowed him to stay himself as long as he did. Assembling the dinosaurs wasn't an angry or hateful task, and it required intense concentration."

Something had been tugging at Peter's consciousness since they'd walked into the room. "They're all carnivores."

The Dog laughed, a short, dry bark. "Yes, they're all carnivores."

Peter sighed. It was no use delaying any longer. His eyes went back to the Tyrannosaurus, and then to the even more terrifying sight resting, as Peter had known it would, between the dinosaur's feet. "It's the rock on the bed, right?"

"Yes," said The Dog, "it's the rock on the bed."

Peter spent the next twenty minutes trying to turn a rock the size of a chicken into a magician. At first, his sisters stood nearby, watching anxiously, but after a minute or two, Peter asked them if they would wait someplace else in the room. "It's hard to do this while you're staring at me," he told them, but that wasn't the real reason. If, by some miracle, he managed to make the rock human again, he wanted Celia and Izzy as far away as possible.

But the longer Peter studied the rock, the less likely it seemed that his sisters had anything to worry about. Sitting on the edge of the bed, Peter felt as though he were once more back on the golf course—except that then he had struggled to summon anything like power, and now he could easily sense the electric current that crackled along every surface in the room. He could feel the power, he could taste it—but he couldn't quite figure out how to use it.

When he stared at the rock, it was just a rock. Once Celia had made him angry, Peter had found it easy enough to change the mushroom back into The Dog, because he had been able to *feel* The Dog inside the mushroom all along. The rock, though, offered Peter nothing; he peered at its uneven gray surface until he had every curve and dent memorized, and yet he could find no hint of the magician underneath. He might, Peter thought, be able to change the rock into some random man, but into the magician? How could he, when he had no idea who the magician was? Peter tried to imagine the sort of person who would create a room like this, but all he could see in his mind's eye was the top-hatted entertainer who had performed card tricks at Celia's eighth birthday party. It wasn't much to go on.

Frustration eventually brought Angry Peter to the surface again. "You're asking me to do something impossible," Peter complained to The Dog, who waited, curled up in a fern near the foot of the bed.

"What do you mean?" said The Dog.

"Are you setting me up?" asked Peter. "What's going to happen when I try to turn him back? Will the spell bounce back on me like it did on him? Is that why you won't change him back yourself?"

The Dog stood up, bringing his face closer to Peter's. "I told you. I tried, and it didn't work. I'm not powerful enough."

"So you keep saying," snapped Peter, "but how do I know that's true?"

"Let's focus on the problem at hand," said The Dog. "Why is it impossible for you to make the magician human again?"

"Because I don't know who he is!" shouted Peter. "How can I change him when I don't know who I'm supposed to be changing him into?"

"Oh," said The Dog, "I should have thought of that. If that's all..." He stood up and stretched, then, tail wagging, trotted toward what Peter thought was a Coelophysis. Stopping in front of it, The Dog performed a strange pantomime: he bent his head, grabbed an invisible something with his teeth, then pulled. His head then ducked down again, and when it bobbed up, he had a picture frame clasped in his jaw. He carried this to Peter.

"How did you...?"

"Invisible dresser," The Dog said. "The magician didn't like the way furniture looked in the jungle."

Peter took the frame, which appeared ordinary enough. Then he turned it over and saw the photograph.

It was a picture of a boy and a dog on the lawn in front of a house. The house had white stucco walls and windows framed in robin's-egg blue. The lawn appeared well cared for, and yellow and pink roses bloomed near the front steps. The boy wore a baseball cap and looked about Peter's age; he had his arm around the dog, as if he was trying to hold the dog still for the photo. It was a nice picture, but nothing exciting.

It took Peter a moment to notice it: those were the

same rabbitlike ears, the same long and pointed snout, the same plumy tail.

"It's you," said Peter.

"Well, duh."

"You seem so...you look really happy."

"You're paying attention to the wrong thing," said The Dog. "Don't look at me. Look at the boy."

Peter did as he was told. "Why am I looking at him?" he asked after a moment of studying the boy's friendly, open face, his laughing eyes, the fringe of dark hair that stuck out from the edge of his cap. Perhaps, Peter thought, this was the magician's son.

For a moment, The Dog just stared at him. Then he said, "You're looking at him because he's the magician, of course."

"He's what?"

"He's the magician."

Peter turned back to the photo, shaken. This was the magician, the enslaver of plants, the wrecker of marriages? The obliterator? Peter had wondered what sort of man the magician was. But the magician wasn't a man at all. He was a boy.

Peter's shock must have been visible on his face, because the next thing he knew, his sisters were at his side.

"What's wrong?" said Celia. "Are you okay?"

"Nothing. Just...nothing. I, uh..."

"Did something scary happen?" asked Izzy. Her gaze flickered toward the rock, then back to Peter.

Even if Peter had wanted to, he wasn't sure he could

have explained what he was feeling. So the magician was a boy. The Dog had told him that it was easier to do magic when you were young. He had also told Peter that magicians didn't last long. Peter should have seen this coming.

But he hadn't. He had envisioned someone who had learned magic when he was young, then spent years constructing this house, these servants, and this life. Peter had imagined the transformation from terrific kid to evil magician as a gradual, decades-long process.

But the magician was Peter's age—younger, maybe.

Mutely, he handed the photo to his sisters. Then he turned back to The Dog. "That was taken before he learned to do magic?"

"The week before, actually," said The Dog.

"How old is he in the picture?"

"Twelve and a half."

Peter cleared his throat, which seemed unaccountably tight. "How old was he when he turned himself into a rock?"

"Thirteen. And three months."

Peter glanced back at the rock. Inside that rock was a boy, a boy just like him. How did it feel to be a rock? The Dog had made it sound as if he had been himself even when he was mushroom: he'd been tired, he'd said; he'd wished he could lie down and go to sleep. Was that how the magician felt? Peter tried to remind himself that the boy captured within that gray rock was the same person who had destroyed someone's home merely because the kids were loud in the pool. But what he saw, looking at the rock, was a fringe of dark hair with laughing eyes peeking out from underneath. A slim arm wrapped around a dog, a body paused in the middle of playing. A boy, nothing but a boy, and now he was a rock, and somewhere, in a house with roses in the yard, his parents must be missing him terribly.

From the moment he had entered this house, Peter had been frightened of what the magician would do to him. But now, for the first time, he pitied the magician, and moved by that pity, he reached out his hand to run it along the rock.

The moment his fingers brushed its surface, he knew he had made a horrible mistake.

Chapter Fourteen

The rock was alive with magic. It zinged through Peter's fingertips and up his arm, making him gasp with pain. From his arm, it raced up his neck before concentrating itself in that particular spot in his head two inches behind his right temple. He felt as if his head had been plugged into an electrical outlet.

And then, though Peter could swear he had done nothing, had thought nothing, the power shot out of him. He sucked in air, realizing only as he did so that it was the first time he'd breathed since he'd touched the rock.

An earth-shattering roar filled the room, followed by screaming.

Next to Peter, The Dog muttered the sort of word that Peter's mother did not allow him to say. The Dog's long face scrunched up as if he was about to do magic.

Peter, although aware of everything around him, felt strange. It was as if he were wrapped in a thick blanket that muffled all sound, all sight, even all emotion, and the only thing that remained clear was the rock that he now clasped between his hands (though he couldn't remember picking it up—when had he done that?). The rock was beautiful, he realized in surprise, as another terrible roar filled the room. How could he have mistaken it for ordinary? Its surface was covered with white and silver speckles that glinted and glimmered, catching every stray bit of light. Its bumps and divots held waves of motion, like an ocean turned to stone. It was perhaps the most beautiful thing Peter had ever seen.

"Peter," said The Dog, "I think we've got a problem." The anxiousness in The Dog's voice irritated Peter because he didn't want to listen to The Dog; he wanted to admire the rock. "I'm trying, but I don't think my magic's going to work against him. I need your help."

The roar came again, followed by Celia shrieking. "We have to run. Come on, Peter. Now!"

Something tugged at Peter's clothes. Peter looked down: Izzy was pulling at his jeans. "Peter? What should we do?"

What does she mean, what should we do? Peter wondered. The right thing to do—the *only* thing to do—was to look at the rock. Cradling the rock to his chest, Peter swatted Izzy's grasping fingers away, shoving her to the ground in the process.

Celia gaped. Izzy started to cry.

"The rock!" shouted The Dog. "I didn't realize—get his hands off the rock!"

But Peter didn't want to let go of the rock. He had sensed the magician's presence in it from the moment he had touched it, and the longer he held it, the stronger his awareness of the magician became. In fact, he thought he might even be able to hear the magician, like a distant echo, calling to him. If Peter could just listen hard enough...

He couldn't finish the thought, because Celia tried to pull his hands off the rock. Peter easily pushed her away. She tackled him again, this time clawing at his shoulders and arms. *Statue,* Peter thought, and Celia froze in place, her fingers still touching his. He started to detangle his body from hers—but at that moment, something launched itself at his side, the force powerful enough that it pushed both Peter and the frozen Celia to the ground.

As Peter fell painfully to his knees, the rock went flying from his grasp. The moment he was no longer touching it, the fog that had enshrouded him lifted, and the anger he had been feeling disappeared, too. Left behind was the knowledge of what he had done. "Izzy...Celia... I'm so—"

Before he could finish his apology, another roar echoed through the room. This time, Peter looked up.

Directly above him, what had been the skeleton of a Tyrannosaurus was rapidly growing muscles and tendons, skin and flesh. The monster's head was already complete, the mighty jaws opening and shutting as though they were relearning the motion they had last practiced millions of years ago. And relearning quickly. As Peter watched aghast, a coat of thick gray scales spread down the dinosaur's short arms, then started across its belly; the ease with which they flowed across the beast's body reminded Peter of spilling water. At least its feet were still bone, Peter reassured himself, but even as he thought it, muscles built bridges from the tibia to the metatarsals, from the metatarsals to the toes. At this rate, the dinosaur would be whole in a matter of minutes.

"What's happening?" Peter yelled, turning to the furry shape that had knocked him to the ground.

The Dog looked at him helplessly. "I didn't know," he said. "The magician must have set up a protective spell that he didn't tell me about. When you touched the rock, it woke up the Tyrannosaurus."

"Can't you make it stop?" Peter demanded. "You've got to do something!"

"I've tried," said The Dog. "But nothing I'm doing is working."

Peter gestured wildly toward the dinosaur. Its knees were now covered in skin. Peter could feel its breath on his head, even smell the stench of ancient meat rotting on its teeth. "You have to stop it!"

"No!" The Dog yelled back. "*You* have to stop it. Or it will kill us all."

The dinosaur roared again.

Peter's eyes swept desperately around the room. Celia was a statue. Izzy lay crying on the ground. There was no time to run. No time to do anything at all.

Peter turned back to the dinosaur. He had no choice.

Freeze, he thought, letting Angry Peter surface. Peter could feel the fury opening a channel in his mind, directing the magic that was present around him to the one small spot in his brain that knew what to do with it. *Freeze,* he thought once more, almost confidently, as he gazed straight up at the now completely resurrected Tyrannosaurus.

Unmoving, the monster stared down at Peter, a

million years of hunger in its pale eyes. For a moment, Peter felt sure that the magic had worked.

Then, as though helping itself at a buffet, the dinosaur bent its massive head toward Izzy.

"Peter!" Izzy screamed. "Help!"

Peter's magic wasn't enough. The monster's jaws were opening to devour his sister.

Panic coiled into a hard knot at the center of Peter's stomach. *Think. Think.* He hadn't been able to freeze the dinosaur, he told himself, but that didn't mean he couldn't use magic at all. If he couldn't stop the dinosaur, was there something else he could do to save Izzy?

Cage! he thought as the Tyrannosaurus's teeth began to close on Izzy's shoulder.

This time, the magic worked. As Peter watched, bars formed out of nothing, crisscrossing the air around Izzy's curled-up form, creating an iron box that contained her and nothing else. The Tyrannosaurus was left with a scrap of striped pajama in its mouth. At first, it didn't understand. It snapped at the bars with its gigantic teeth; then, to Peter's horror, it picked up the cage in its mouth, shaking it from side to side while Izzy rattled violently within. When that didn't free its meal, the dinosaur roared and tossed the cage to the ground twenty feet from where Peter stood, Izzy still as a rag doll inside it.

Still hungry, the dinosaur turned toward the other children. Hunting like a snake, it lunged at them with its whole body, but this time, Peter was prepared. *Cage!* he thought again, and a cage appeared around Peter, Celia, and The Dog. The Tyrannosaurus's jaws opened wide: it looked as though it was going to try to swallow them cage and all, and Peter, staring up the enormous tunnel of its throat, wondered if it might succeed. As the beast fastened its teeth onto the metal bars, Peter realized that it could toss the three of them as easily as tiny Izzy. *Heavy,* Peter thought, and when the monster pulled its head up a moment later, the cage didn't move.

The Tyrannosaurus rattled the bars, roaring its frustration. Then it rocked back on its haunches to stare malevolently at them, a cat watching a mouse-hole, just daring the mice to try to escape.

They were, for the moment, safe. Inside the cage, Peter felt his legs give out beneath him; shuddering, he fell to the dirt floor.

"Well," The Dog said, "that wasn't perhaps the tidiest solution, but still, I'm impressed. Wish I'd thought of it."

"What..." Peter's tongue felt heavy in his mouth; he was so tired he could barely speak. "What's wrong with me?"

"Too much magic," said The Dog. "It's exhausted you."

"Izzy...," said Peter, too tired to say more.

The Dog looked over to where Izzy lay. Worry flickered across his face. Like Peter, he must have noticed that Izzy hadn't moved since being thrown by the dinosaur. "Izzy?" The Dog called out. "Are you okay?"

For a moment, everything was silent, and Peter's breath caught in his chest. Then Izzy's small blond head popped up. "Is it safe to move?"

"Yes, it's safe to move," said The Dog. "For now, anyway."

"Oh, good," said Izzy. "I was playing dead. I know that works with bears. I saw it once on the Discovery Channel."

"Are you hurt?" asked The Dog.

"My head got banged," said Izzy. "But I'm okay. Are Petey and Celia all right?"

"Peter's good," said The Dog. "He's just tired. And Celia's still frozen, but otherwise she's fine."

Peter turned to The Dog. "Can't you bring her here?" he said, too quietly for Izzy to hear.

"I could if I had to," said The Dog, "but I think I should conserve any power I have left until we come up with a plan. That's why I haven't unfrozen Celia, either. We're not out of this mess yet."

"No, not yet," said Peter. The Tyrannosaurus might be as still as the fossilized bones surrounding them, but there was no ignoring its relentless gaze. "Why couldn't I stop it?" Peter asked. Of everything that had happened, this was the thing that bothered him most. He had felt that magic travel through him. It should've worked, and it hadn't.

The Dog frowned. "I don't know why. If the magician were here, he'd be more powerful than you are by far, but that must have been an old spell, a trap—it should have been weaker."

Peter looked at the rock, which had fallen to the ground when The Dog had pushed him and now lay inside the cage. Peter remembered how he had felt when he had touched it; how, for those moments, he had believed that the rock was only thing in the world that mattered. He remembered, too, his sense of the magician calling him. Had there really been a voice?

"Do you have enough power to get us all out of here?" he asked The Dog. "I mean, could you transport us? Just out of the house, maybe?"

The Dog shook his head. "I'm sorry. I've done too much magic already. It would be dangerous for me to move three people."

"So what are we going to do?" said Peter.

"Wait, I guess," said The Dog. "We're safe enough in here, and if I can get some sleep, I'll be able to move us tomorrow."

"But my mother!" cried Peter. "She won't know where we are! She'll be worried sick!"

"Not much we can do about that," said The Dog.

"Peter?" Izzy called out now from where she sat cross-legged in her own cage.

"Yes?"

"I know you like dinosaurs a lot. But I don't think I like them so much. I'm sorry."

Izzy was apologizing to him. Izzy, whom Peter had brought into this danger; Izzy, who would have waited in the hallway if Peter had told her to. Peter stared down once more at the rock that had caused all this trouble. It was just a plain rock now: no glinting diamond speckles, no frozen oceans caught within it. How strange that it had looked so different when he was touching it! It had felt almost as if the magician had really been there! But of course the rock *was* the magician, he reminded himself.

And suddenly he understood what he had to do.

"Listen," Peter said to The Dog, "you may need to remind me."

The Dog's ears flattened. "Remind you of what?"

"Remind me of who I am."

"What are you talking about?"

Peter didn't answer. He had a plan, and the plan required that he do something that terrified him to his core. *No point in thinking about it,* he told himself. That was what his father would say, if he were here. *Everyone feels fear, kid,* his father had said when Peter had once asked him how it felt to fly planes into a war. *But the fear isn't what matters. It's the choices you make when you're afraid that matter; that's what you can control.*

Peter made a choice. He reached out and touched the rock. And this time, when he sensed the magician calling, he let the sound carry him where it wanted him to go.

Chapter Fifteen

Peter was lying on his back, and his eyes were open. He was sure of that last fact because when he blinked, darkness descended like a curtain over a stage. Yes, he thought, his eyes must be open, but how was he to make sense of the dull gray surface in front of him, a surface like nothing he had ever seen? When he breathed, the air tasted metallic and stale; and the silence that surrounded him was so absolute that he thought if he listened hard enough, he might even hear the nervous thud of his heart in his chest. He couldn't remember where he was or how he had gotten here. In fact, he could remember very little. Still. He might not remember much, but there were things he *knew,* and one thing he knew was that he ought to feel afraid. And he did.

He sat up slowly, but the view didn't change: more gray, as what had been ceiling curved down to become the walls and then the floor. It was both like a cave and not like a cave, because even in caves, you could tell what was up and what was down. Here everything was the same, so that if the room rolled one way or another, you would never notice. Peter felt as if he were in a cold gray egg.

As if reading his thoughts, a voice asked, "Do you like it here, Peter?" The sound bounced hollowly from the surrounding walls.

Peter jumped to his feet and whirled around. There, behind him, was a boy with dark hair and a thin, clever face. The boy was smiling at him, but the smile made Peter shiver.

"I didn't hear you," Peter said.

"That's because there was nothing to hear," said the boy. "I didn't feel like breathing, and I only do things I feel like doing when I'm here."

"Huh?"

The boy laughed. "You'll understand soon enough, Peter."

That was twice now the boy had said Peter's name. "Umm...do I know you? I can't quite remember...do you know where I am?" *Or who I am,* he wanted to add, but instinct warned him against revealing how little he knew.

"Sure you know me," the boy said. "I can't tell you how glad I am to see you."

"Are we friends?" asked Peter doubtfully.

"Oh, yes," said the boy. "You're my best friend." And he put his arm around Peter's shoulders and squeezed.

It hurt a bit, that hug, but Peter didn't complain. "I think...I think I'd like to go home," he said instead, even though he couldn't remember exactly where home was.

"Oh, I'm afraid that's not going to be possible." The boy sounded sympathetic, but laughter curled the corners of his mouth. Peter looked around once more for a way out, but the walls of the stone egg were smooth, unbroken by crack or crevice. How on earth had he gotten in here in the first place? How had either of them gotten in here? An answer arrived in his head, like a letter dropping into a mail slot: he had gotten here by making a decision.

"I'm supposed to be doing something," Peter said to the boy. "I'm sure of it. Do you know what it is?"

"You're supposed to be here with me."

"No, I—"

"Let me show what I can do," the boy interrupted. "You'll think this fun." And then an amazing thing happened. Though the boy did not move, a remote control appeared in his hand, and when Peter looked down, he found one clenched in his palm as well. A whirring noise began to echo against the walls: at Peter's feet were parked two small race cars, one red, one blue. "Ready, set, go!" shouted the boy, and the blue car drove off with a roar. It zoomed across the floor, went straight up the wall, and, to Peter's astonishment, sped across the ceiling. In less time than it would take to count to ten, it had circled the cave and was back at Peter's feet.

"I won!" crowed the boy. "Although that was far too easy. You never even touched a button on your remote."

"How did it drive on the ceiling?" asked Peter.

"I told you. I make the rules in here, and one of my rules is that cars can race on the ceiling. Now, focus this time. I haven't had anyone to race before today, and racing by yourself is boring, boring, boring. Ready, set—"

"I don't want to race," said Peter. He dropped his remote to the ground, where it clanged against the rock.

The boy's eyes flashed, and all pretense of niceness disappeared. "I don't remember asking what you wanted."

"I thought we were friends," said Peter.

"Oh, yes," said the boy. "We're friends. And that's why you have to do what I tell you. That's one of my rules, too."

He had come here by choice, Peter reminded himself. He might not know who he was or why he had chosen this, but nonetheless the decision had been his own. "No," he said.

"Listen here," said the boy, "this is my place...."

Listen. The moment Peter heard that word, he knew it was the thing he was supposed to be doing. *Listen. Listen.* Next to him, the boy kept talking, but Peter shut out his voice, struggling to hear what might be behind it, outside these enclosing gray walls. At first, he heard only that muffling silence. Then he listened harder.

Peter! Peter!

Was it his imagination? Or was someone calling his name?

Can you hear me? We're here, Petey!

Petey. Someone called him Petey. Someone he loved.

"Izzy," he said, under his breath, and he remembered everything. The Dog must have transported her to the bigger cage if Peter could hear her through the rock, he realized.

The boy was still talking.

"You're the magician," Peter said. "I'm in the rock with you, aren't I?"

The cars and remotes disappeared, and a change came over the boy, too. He seemed to grow, three or four inches at least; his eyes darkened, and his expression became fierce and cold. He didn't look like a boy anymore: whatever had been young in his face disappeared.

"Yes," said the boy, and even his voice was more dangerous somehow. "I'm the magician. And I'd like very much to know what you're doing in my house."

Peter tried to speak, but all that came out was a squeak. He cleared his throat and tried again. "I want to help you," he choked out. "To make you human. That's why I touched the rock again. I could feel you the first time I touched it, and I wanted to explain why I was here so you would tell me how to stop the Tyrannosaurus."

"You're here to make me human again?" The magician's eyebrows shot up.

"Yes."

"Because...? Hmm. Let me think. Because you're just a nice kid who spends his time rescuing his fellow magicians in their moments of need? That's it, right?"

Peter thought frantically. When he had decided to touch the rock, he had imagined bargaining with the magician, explaining that he would make the magician human again only if the magician would bring his father back. It had seemed like a logical plan at the time, but here, under the magician's cold gaze, Peter felt less sure. Still, he had to try.

"My father...He's at war. I don't have enough power to bring him home." Peter stumbled over his words. "I thought maybe you—"

"That's what I thought," said the magician. "You're here to steal my magic. I may be a rock at the moment, but I'm not going to allow that."

Remembering that the magician was a rock gave Peter a trickle of courage. "I'm not here to steal your magic. I'm here to help you. You're powerless right now, and you need me if you want to change back."

The magician snarled in fury, the sound echoing off the cave's walls until Peter had to cover his ears and drop to his knees. "I'm powerless, huh? Just see what I can do." The magician smiled, and electricity began to gather in Peter's head, just as it had when he had first touched the rock: he had the same sense of enormous power rushing through his body, his brain nothing but a pain-filled conduit. In the distance, he could hear the muffled sounds of The Dog barking, his sisters screaming. And another sound...it was his own voice, shrieking.

And then the power shot out of him.

"What...what did you do?" Peter asked as soon as he could speak again.

"Woke up the rest of the dinosaurs," the magician said smugly.

"I don't understand," said Peter.

"You're not supposed to understand," said the magician. "Instead of trying, why don't you just listen to your little sisters cry for help while a hundred or more predators attack them? Your cage was very clever. But the Dromaeosauruses, for instance, are small enough to fit between the bars."

A moment before, Peter had been able to hear his sisters only when he concentrated fully on listening, and even then the sounds he'd heard had been muffled. Now, though, their voices filled the cave, as if they were standing next to him.

"Do something, Dog!" Celia cried. "Oh, please, can't you do something?"

The Dog grunted. "I'm trying. There's just so many! A net over the cage... that might—but—"

Izzy screamed, "It's over your head, Celia!"

"Use the stick!" The Dog shouted. "Izzy, get behind me!"

Peter couldn't bear it. He launched himself against the cave's walls, pounding so hard his knuckles began to bleed.

The magician laughed.

Peter turned, his fists still raised.

"That won't do," said the magician. "No violence in my rock." Like that, Peter's body froze. The magician's eyes narrowed, and the voices of Peter's sisters disappeared. "So do you still think I'm powerless? How do you feel now, paralyzed and at my mercy? Would you like to see what else I can do?"

Though Peter didn't close his eyes, though he did nothing at all, everything changed. He was no longer in the cave. Instead, he was standing on a dusty road in a strange brown land, a road lined with dilapidated houses, most of which had broken windows. It was so hot that the air rippled. In front of Peter, a cluster of dark-haired men bent over something. Peter didn't remember deciding to move, yet he found himself walking toward them. He couldn't understand the words floating back to him; *not English*, he thought in the corner of his mind still capable of logic.

Then he heard the thrum of an approaching plane. And because in the dark hours of the night he had imagined this moment so many times, he knew what would happen next.

The men shifted, and a large rocket launcher became visible on the ground. *Run,* Peter told his legs, though he didn't know whether he meant to run toward the men, to try to stop them, or run away, so he wouldn't have to see what was about to occur. Either way, his legs didn't listen, just continued their calm walk forward, even as tears began to streak down his cheeks.

I'm about to watch my father die, Peter thought. Because there was no question in his mind that his father was piloting the F-16 growing larger by the second on the horizon.

But why? Despite the men, the heat, the deafening roar of the airplane, Peter tried to shut out everything going on around him and instead replay what had happened since he had woken up in the cave. The magician had pretended to be his friend. He had wanted to race cars. He had awakened the dinosaurs to attack Peter's sisters. And now he was killing Peter's father. Why?

Based on the sound, the plane was almost directly above him. The men with the rocket were shouting now, their excitement and fear audible despite the harsh foreign words. Peter's feet stopped. That must mean he was perfectly positioned to witness his father's death.

Why? Because the magician wanted to distract Peter—to keep him from noticing something. Which must mean that there was something Peter could do to end this; the magician must not be as all-powerful as he seemed.

The plane was overhead. The rocket boomed. There was a whistle like a dragon hissing, and flame streaked through the sky.

You can't find the right answers unless you ask the right questions, Peter's father always said. How had the magician known about Peter's worst nightmare, which he was living through now? Why were all the details exactly the way Peter had imagined them when his fears took over in the night? For that matter, how did the magician know about Peter's sisters, about the cage? Why hadn't the magician changed himself back if he was capable of magic on this scale?

Peter could think of only one answer: because the magician was inside his mind, reading his thoughts and using his magic. Which meant that maybe, just maybe, none of what seemed to be happening now was real.

The explosion when the rocket hit F-16 was deafening. The echo of it was still in Peter's ears as pieces of the plane began to rain down on the road. Peter watched jagged hunks of metal fall through the azure sky; fear seemed to slow down time, so that to Peter's eyes, everything appeared to be drifting earthward. It all fell so slowly, Peter thought; it seemed as if a clever boy could run from spot to spot and catch each sliver of the wreckage. Through a mist of ashy snowflakes, a seat dropped almost wholly intact, its upholstery ablaze. And there. Wasn't that his father's helmet, tumbling through the smoky haze? In front of Peter, the men scattered, some running into houses, others climbing into a faded blue pickup truck.

Ask the right questions. What was the first thing Peter had done when he had awoken in the rock? He had opened his eyes, he thought, though something about that moment had felt wrong. So now he would open his eyes again.

Peter's eyelids felt heavy, as though they were battling his intention. Still, Peter forced them to work. Close, open. Close, open. At first the carnage in the desert was all he could see. Close, open. A plane's wing at an unnatural angle in the sand. *Concentrate. Concentrate harder.* Close, open. And then, a miracle. The inside of the cave, the magician staring at him, furious.

It was not enough, though. Close, open. Close, open. *Focus,* Peter told himself. His sisters' lives might depend upon it.

He tried one more time. Close, open. And this time, when he opened his eyes, he saw them: his own hands gripping the rock. As they had been this whole time, he now understood. He had never been in the rock; he had been standing here, in the magician's bedroom, while the magician used Peter's senses against him, stealing Peter's power and lodging himself like a parasite in Peter's mind. Next to Peter, The Dog was growling and Celia was yelling angrily. From every side came the high-pitched, bloodthirsty calls of dinosaurs. Peter's knees almost buckled as Izzy fastened herself around his legs, crying.

He ignored it all; waking himself from the magician's

dream was only half of what he must do. The magician had used Peter's mind, but didn't conduits flow both ways? Peter had felt the magician's power when he'd touched the rock before; it must be there now, literally at his fingertips. This was the knowledge the magician had been distracting him from.

There was no need to let his anger build this time.

Stop, dinosaurs! Peter thought, and like that, magic flooded from the rock through his body, more magic than when the magician had awakened the Tyrannosaurus or the other predators, more magic than Peter had ever felt or imagined.

The power shot out of him, leaving what? *Pain,* Peter thought. *Grief.* Then emptiness. Peter watched his hands drop the rock; as it fell to the ground, he, too, fell, helpless to stop himself. But before he hit the dirt, Izzy's arms on his legs loosened, her crying abruptly ceasing. Celia cheered, and even The Dog let out a howl of triumph. *It must have worked,* Peter thought. He had stopped the dinosaurs, but he found it hard to care. The ground was cool and welcome against his face, and he was grateful for the blackness that swallowed him.

Chapter Sixteen

Peter was in the soup.

The soup was black and liquid and murky. It was neither hot nor cold; it was just soup, thick enough that even a strong boy couldn't swim through it. And a boy like Peter—well, he didn't stand a chance.

Occasionally, flickers of the outside world broke through. The pull of being dragged across a dirt floor. The discomfort of being slung across bony shoulders. And then, oddly, the cool of the desert wind rushing past his face. But these were flickers only, not enough to awaken Peter's interest.

The truth was, Peter *liked* the soup. It was quiet in the darkness, and peaceful, too, in its own way. No one asked anything of him; no one needed him to do, or be, anything. Most importantly, there were no roaring dinosaurs or terrified sisters in the soup. No magician with cruel eyes. No falling pieces of plane.

He thought he might stay in the soup forever.

A voice was talking. Peter's voice.

"Yeah, I threw up three times. I don't feel so good."

A low murmur...could that really be his mother?

"Uh-huh. I think I'd better stay home today. I was awake all night...."

More words, then cool lips brushing his forehead, the smell of citrus in his nose. The smell was enough to stir a flash of awareness in him; for a moment, he floated closer to the soup's surface. Emotion tugged at him. But he didn't want to feel, so he didn't.

His voice was speaking again. "Poor Izzy. And Celia, too, huh? I can't believe we all got sick at once. Sure, I'll keep an eye on them while you're gone. Don't worry, Mom—you go teach. We'll be okay without you."

Then it was quiet again. With relief, Peter slipped downward once more.

Time passed.

"Peter...Peter...Please wake up, Peter! It's getting late. We need to talk to you. Peter!"

The voice was insistent, the frantic words coiling around and around Peter and dragging him upward. *Leave me alone!* he wanted to tell Celia, but you can't speak when you're in the soup. Inside his own head, he curled into a ball, humming softly, trying to drown out her voice.

"Peter? Please, Peter? When are you going to wake up?"

More darkness.

This time, it wasn't words that pulled him up. Something cold was on his knees. Something he couldn't ignore.

He knew that feeling, he thought. *Izzy.* Of course. Izzy's toes. She must be curled up next to him, her feet on his legs.

But Izzy didn't belong in the soup. And he couldn't be in the soup if Izzy was next to him.

Reluctantly, he opened his eyes.

Light came flooding in. He blinked against the brightness, and what had been blotches of color resolved into familiar sights. The water stain on his bedroom ceiling, which he'd stared at as he'd gone to sleep for the past six months. The dark-blue flannel of his pajamas (had his sisters put them on him?). The top of Izzy's blond head. Although he could feel magic buzzing on every surface, jangling his nerves and demanding his attention, he told himself to ignore it. At least the room was silent. Maybe, he thought, he would be able to handle this.

And then suddenly Celia's face was inches from his own, her expression incredulous. "You're awake!" she shouted, her voice so loud after the quiet of the soup that Peter wanted to clap his hands over his ears. "It's about time! I didn't think you were ever going to open your eyes. Mom's going to be here in a couple of hours, and we've still got to figure out what to do about the rock, and Henry, and…and…" Out of nowhere, Celia burst into tears.

Then Izzy sat up, and The Dog put his paws on the bed, and the three anxious faces stared down at Peter. Anxious, and expectant, too, Peter thought; he had been awake for a few seconds only, and already they wanted something from him. If only he could go back into that calm darkness!

"I'm so happy you're awake!" said Izzy. Her small

arms wrapped around him, squeezing. "No matter what we did, you wouldn't wake up."

Something wet shoved itself into Peter's elbow. "Glad to see you with your eyes open, Peter," said The Dog.

Peter pushed himself into a sitting position. "Why is Celia crying?" he asked, or tried to, anyway. His voice, rusty from disuse, was barely audible even to his own ears.

"Huh?" said The Dog.

"Why is Celia crying?" Peter repeated, and this time his words shot out more loudly than he intended, loudly enough that Celia's tears abruptly stopped and Izzy's smile disappeared from her face.

"She's crying because she was worried about you," said The Dog. "We were all worried about you. Will you tell us what happened?"

He couldn't talk to them, Peter thought. Not yet. There was something he had to do first.

"I need a minute alone," he said.

"But, Peter—" said Celia.

"I want to get dressed!" Peter said. At least his pajamas gave him an excuse.

"Oh," said Izzy, and she obediently moved toward the door. Celia, too, followed, but her still-wet eyes lingered on Peter's face, questioning.

The Dog, on the other hand, was staring at Peter's closet. "Peter, we should explain—"

"Please?" said Peter, his voice cracking. "I just... I want a minute alone. To change."

The Dog looked at Peter, looked back at the closet, then stood up. "Okay. If that's what you want."

The door swung closed; Peter was by himself. He hurried to his desk and turned on his computer; while it powered up, he grabbed the first pair of shorts he could find in his drawer. As he pulled them on, the background image on his desktop came into focus: his father, dressed in his air force uniform, smiling back at him. Peter clicked on his email icon. And waited.

The first message to load was from a friend from New Jersey. The second was an update from a NASA kids' site. And then it was there. The message Peter's father sent each evening; the one that, because of the time difference, showed up on Peter's computer in the morning. Peter clicked it open, skimming the words about a storm in the desert; a card game his father had planned for later that night. It wasn't much, but it was enough to know that his father had been alive to send it, that the images he had seen of his father's death had been the magician's creation and nothing else.

It had seemed so real. So very, very real. He could still see his father's helmet falling from the sky.

"Are you dressed yet?" Celia called from outside Peter's door.

Peter fought an urge to use the magic he could feel vibrating around him to think himself invisible. His sisters and The Dog would find the room empty; they would hurry off to look for him while he went back to sleep. Instead, he shut his computer down, then sprang to his feet. "Just a second," he said. Yanking open his closet, he reached for a shirt.

And froze. From within the closet, the mouse who was also a waiter stared back at him, unblinking.

The mouse-waiter made no immediate move. So Peter didn't move, either. Instead, he just stood there, trying to make sense of what he was seeing. The waiter didn't seem aggressive; in fact, he mostly looked scared. "Umm, Dog?" Peter said after a moment or two had passed. "Could you, um, come here?"

The Dog, Celia, and Izzy flew into the room. Izzy spoke first. "You found Henry!"

"Why is the waiter in my closet?"

The Dog shook his nose exasperatedly. "Don't blame me. This one is all on your sisters. After the dinosaurs froze, we dragged you into the hallway. We were stuck there, discussing what to do next, when the waiter—"

"Henry," Izzy interrupted. "He didn't have a name, so I gave him one. And he says he likes it."

The Dog sighed. "When *Henry* came along. Apparently you'd left him walking the hallway looking for the magician's open door. Did you know he would keep going until someone told him otherwise? I think he was pretty relieved to stumble on us."

"He asked if he could help," said Izzy, "and I told him we needed a ride home, so he picked you up and carried you on his shoulders to this ginormous garage, and then he drove us home. And, Peter, you should have seen the car he drove us in. It's little and yellow, and it doesn't have a roof. And Henry drives it very fast, and he swerves around a lot. He's really fun. I think he should live in your closet forever."

The story made sense of what Peter remembered from being in the soup. It also explained how they had gotten home, which he probably should have wondered about but hadn't; he had been too worried about his father. Still…"Why is he in my closet? I mean, why doesn't he come out?"

"He likes it in there," said Celia. "He says he likes places that are quiet and dark."

The waiter, who still hadn't spoken, nodded.

"And the magician?" Peter asked. "What did you do with the rock? Did you just leave it there?"

"Oh, no," said Celia. "We brought it with us. It's in the backyard. I put it under the birdbath."

"It's *here*?"

Celia's smile faded. "I was trying to help. I thought that this way you wouldn't have to go back to the magician's house to make him human again. And I was careful not to touch it after I saw what it did to you. I carried it wrapped in my shirt."

"I'm not trying to make him human again," snapped Peter.

"But what about Dad?" asked Celia. "I thought you were going to change the magician so he would help you bring Dad back."

"That was before I went into the rock," Peter said, "and saw what he was like. He'll never help us with Dad. And even if he would, I wouldn't make him human again. Not ever."

In front of him, The Dog dropped to his haunches and, to Peter and his sisters' shock, began to yowl. The heart-wrenching sound filled Peter's room. Then The Dog turned and stalked out the door.

I could wish for a rocket ship, Peter thought. It would

carry him into space. He could see Jupiter and Mars—and leave all this behind.

For the rest of the afternoon, The Dog didn't speak to anyone. He curled up on the mat by the back door and refused to move, his long, warty nose resting miserably on the carpet. After trying everything they could think of to coax him from his silence, the children held a hasty conference in the kitchen.

"Do you think he's sick?" asked Izzy. "Why won't he talk to us?"

"He's not sick," declared Celia. "He's mad. At Peter. That's why he won't talk. Peter could help him if he wanted to."

The Dog was not the only one who was mad at Peter. Peter and Celia had been arguing ever since Peter's announcement. "I can't change the magician," Peter repeated now, for the fourth or fifth time.

"You can't or you won't?"

"I won't," Peter admitted.

Celia shook her head, her curls bobbing wildly. "No matter how evil he is, it's still the right thing to do if it means Dad will be home."

"He'll hurt you and Izzy," said Peter.

"I don't care."

"Well, I do."

For a moment, they glared at each other. Then Celia's gaze dropped to the floor. "If the magician won't help, do you think you could become powerful enough to bring Dad home yourself?"

Peter felt his hands clench into fists. "I'm not doing any more magic." Only Izzy's presence kept him from shouting.

A tear slid down Celia's face. "But I miss him."

"No." Without another word, Peter stomped down the hallway to the living room, then turned on the TV with the volume up high to make it clear that he was done with conversation. Eventually, Celia and Izzy joined him, all three staring at a program that none of them was interested in.

And that was where Peter's mother found them when she arrived home from work, her arms weighed down with grocery bags. She took one look at their unhappy faces, and her lips pursed with worry. She had called several times during the day: first Celia and then Peter had explained that everyone was feeling better; no, she didn't need to hurry home from work; it just seemed to be a short-lived flu, really. But Peter could tell by the way she stood there, staring at them, that she knew something was wrong.

For a moment, all thought of magic, of The Dog, even of his father slid from Peter's mind. The only thing that mattered was reassuring his mom.

"Let me take those," he said, grabbing the grocery bags. "Izzy, Celia—you want to help me unload?"

Izzy and Celia jumped up from the couch. "Mmm," said Celia, poking around in one of the bags. "You bought stuff for chicken noodle soup."

"Can I help make it?" asked Izzy.

"Yes," said Peter's mom, looking between them with confusion. "If you're feeling better?"

"Much better," said Izzy.

"We're good now," added Celia.

Peter could see the doubt in his mother's face, but for the rest of the evening, the children acted as though everything were fine, and Peter's mother acted as though everything were fine, too: all in all, it would have seemed as if they were a perfectly normal family if it hadn't been for The Dog lying motionless on the doormat. Peter thought his mother hadn't noticed until he went to tell her good night.

"Did you feed the dog?" she asked.

"Yes," said Peter. He didn't add that The Dog hadn't yet touched his food.

"I don't think I've seen him get up since I got home. Do you think he's okay?"

"I don't know," said Peter. "He's been really quiet today." This, at least, was the truth.

Peter's mom frowned. "Let's see how he is tomorrow. If he's still not acting like himself, we can call that young man—Timothy."

"Sounds good, Mom."

"I hope...I hope you're feeling okay, honey."

"I'm fine. Thanks."

Peter's mom reached out and smoothed his hair. "Is there anything you want to talk to me about?" she asked. "I know you try to take care of me and your sisters when your dad is gone. But you know I'm here for you if you need me, don't you?"

Peter felt something twist painfully in his chest. "I know."

Peter crawled into bed wanting nothing more than to fall asleep quickly. Instead, as he lay there, tossing and turning every few minutes, he found himself forced to confront the truth he had been avoiding all day. The truth that he wouldn't tell his sisters. That he could barely admit to himself.

He had told Celia that he wouldn't change the magician back because he didn't think the magician would help them and because he was scared of what the magician would do. And neither of these was a lie, exactly. But the hard and ugly truth that faced Peter now, lying in his bed, was that it wasn't just these facts that kept him from making the magician human. It was the fear of what performing more magic might do to Peter himself.

How could he explain to Celia what he had seen when he looked at the magician, who no longer bore any resemblance at all to the boy in the photograph The Dog had shown him? A year, perhaps less, and that might be Peter, too. How could Peter tell Celia that as much as he wanted to save his father, he didn't want to pay the price?

Every time Peter closed his eyes, he saw the magician's face before him, until he finally fell into a restless, dream-filled sleep.

He woke up some hours later to the sensation that he was being watched. He turned his head to find two large, glowing eyes inches from his.

"Hey!" he said.

"It's just me," said The Dog. "I didn't mean to startle you."

"If you don't mean to startle me, you shouldn't stare at me in the middle of the night." Relieved to see The Dog up, Peter almost reached out to scratch his ears but then thought better of it. "Are you feeling better?"

The Dog thumped his tail against the floor. "I didn't come in here to discuss me. I put a spell on your mom so we could talk without waking her up. I've been thinking all day, and there's something I need to tell you."

"What?"

The Dog opened his mouth as if to speak, then closed it again. When he finally spoke, he seemed to have changed his mind about what he wanted to say. "Can I ask you something first? Do you know how you've managed to stay you?"

Chapter Seventeen

"What do you mean, how I've stayed me?" Peter asked.

"Peter, do you want to do more magic?" The Dog asked.

"I...I..." Peter's chin dropped to his chest. "More than anything." It was a relief to finally say the words aloud. "It's like an ache inside me, wanting to do magic. All I can think about is how it felt to fly last night. It was the most amazing thing I've ever done. I felt so powerful. And there are so many other things I could do, too, a thousand big and little things; they've been eating away at me from the moment I opened my eyes today."

"Why don't you just do magic, then?" said The Dog. "If you want to so much. What's stopping you?"

Peter looked at The Dog in despair. "Because I know what's going to happen. Izzy was right all along. I'm going to end up just like your master, aren't I?"

"I don't know," said The Dog. "You haven't done a single spell today, have you?"

"No," said Peter. "But it was all I thought about. And I can feel the anger in me still; I spent all day trying to keep myself from losing my temper. The magic, the anger: they're a part of me now, aren't they?"

The Dog looked as if he wanted to disagree—but then he slowly nodded. "I think so, but maybe I'm wrong. You've known how to do magic for two days. By the time my old master had known for that long, he'd already left home, and he never looked back. What I know about magic, I know mostly from watching him. So maybe you're different. Maybe your story will have a happier ending." He growled, a miserable sort of rumbling that Peter hadn't heard from him before. "I hope so, at any rate."

Ever since Peter had realized the magician was actually a boy, a question had been nagging at him. "How did your master learn magic? Did somebody teach him?"

"Oh, no. I imagine you're the first person who's ever been *taught* magic. My master figured it out."

"What do you mean, he figured it out?"

"He lost his temper. Which kids do; everybody does. But he was the right age, and his mind, like yours, had a certain aptitude for magic. He was arguing with his mother, and instead of storming off to his room the way he would have on another day, he made the kitchen ceiling collapse onto her."

Peter tried to imagine this, but all he could see was his own mother's face. "Was she...?"

"His mother was okay," said The Dog. "Bruised and scraped, mostly. My master wasn't so lucky. He knew what he'd done, and at first he felt terribly guilty, but within an hour, he couldn't help himself: he had to try it again. By that night, he'd made it so I could talk. By the next morning, we were on a flying carpet headed west, and he was already a different person."

Peter shivered, remembering the boy in the rock. "Celia wants me to practice magic until I'm powerful enough to bring my dad home myself."

The Dog's tail swished restlessly from side to side. "That was actually what I wanted to talk to you about. The reason I woke you up, I mean."

For a moment, Peter let himself feel hope. Had The Dog thought of another way to help his father?

"I haven't been as honest as I should have," The Dog continued. "I told you the magician was powerful enough to bring your dad home. And I wasn't lying, not exactly. But there was something I didn't explain. Even magic has its limits. You can use magic to make a bone out of a twig, or to make people out of plants. You can use it to dig fossils out of the ground or learn to fly. You can even use it to bring a man from one side of the world to another."

"So what are the limits?" Peter asked. He could sense that something bad was coming.

"You can do all those things," said The Dog, "because magic is about altering physical details. Remember how I told you that you could change a ficus into a man, but he'd still be a ficus in his heart? Magic can do a lot, but it can't transform someone's essence."

"What does this have to do with my dad?" But even as Peter said the words, he saw his father's face that last morning, the flash of frustration when Peter told him he wished he didn't have to go. *No*, he thought now. *No. No.* He felt an urge to bury his head beneath his pillow so he wouldn't have to hear what The Dog was about to say.

For a long moment, The Dog just stared at Peter, his eyes dark and solemn. "I think you already know what this has to do with your father. Magic could bring him back. But it couldn't change who he is."

"I don't want to change who he is," said Peter.

"But, Peter," The Dog said, "your father chose to become an air force pilot. Flying for the air force—isn't that a part of who he is?"

It started as a roaring in the distance, like the crash of a river against its banks during a storm. And then the sound grew louder, and louder still, until it was all Peter could hear. There was The Dog in front of him, his tail down, his mouth moving. There was Peter's familiar room, the room he had found in the magician's house. Nothing had changed, had it? Except that that terrible roar echoed in Peter's head and changed it all.

He might find a way to bring his father home. But no matter what he did, no matter what he sacrificed, he couldn't make his father stay. That was what The Dog was telling him.

"I wanted to explain," said The Dog, his voice distant and small, "because I think what I did to you was wrong. I didn't lie, exactly, but I misled you. And you're a good kid, a genuinely good kid. You don't deserve the fate you're getting. It was only that I wanted to save my master—"

And then Angry Peter broke loose. This time, there was no one to stop him because Normal Peter didn't care. Normal Peter was angry, too.

In his mind's eye, Peter saw The Dog rising up, up, up. And he thought it.

The Dog's eyes widened as he shot toward the ceiling. "Hey! What are you—"

Peter thought, and The Dog's voice disappeared, as if the Mute button had been pushed on the TV. Pinned to the ceiling, The Dog tried to speak, but no words came out: he twisted and turned his long snout, but nothing happened.

Peter heard a gasp from the doorway. Looking back, he saw his sisters gazing up at The Dog with horror.

"What are you doing here?" he demanded.

"I heard The Dog shout," said Celia. "What's going on? Why is he up there?"

"He's up there because I want him there," said Peter.

"Why?" said Izzy. "I thought you liked him."

Peter heard The Dog's voice in his head again: *Isn't that a part of who he is?* "You were wrong."

Celia grabbed Peter's hand. "This is just the bad magic talking. You can't do this. If you hurt The Dog, he'll never be able to convince the magician to bring Dad home. You just need to transform the magician, and then—"

"Enough about the magician!" said Peter, pushing Celia's hand away. "It's all you talk about. You don't care if doing magic will make me evil. You don't care if I'm going to end up a rock. All you care about—all any of you care about!—is getting what you want." Suddenly Peter knew what he needed to do. "You want the magician back so badly? I'll do it. And then maybe you'll see why I didn't want to change him."

Peter thought, and the rock appeared in the center of the room. Celia gasped, and Izzy's hands flew to her mouth.

Peter remembered the boy he had seen in the cave; then, holding that memory, he studied the rock, discovering bits and pieces of that same boy in its whorls of gray and silver. Perhaps it was Peter's anger, perhaps it was practice, but he was far more powerful than he had been yesterday, he realized as the magic flooded through him.

And Peter thought the rock back into the magician.

Standing there on the carpet, the magician gazed around the room in astonishment. Then a triumphant grin split his face.

"Well, Peter Lubinsky, you did come through for me after all!" he crowed. "I thought after you got out of my trap yesterday that I was stuck in that rock forever. But I guess you can never underestimate a person's stupidity."

"You think I'm stupid?" said Peter. He thought he had transformed the magician because he was angry at Celia, but now he realized what had really driven him: he wanted someone to fight. "I think you're foolish to still be standing there. I brought you back so that I could show what real power is."

The magician raised one eyebrow. Peter braced himself for a spell. But the boy opposite him just laughed. "You've changed! Yesterday you were just a kid who could do magic. But today you're a magician. What fun! I love a good fight with another magician. Let's see: shall I start with you, or with the spectators?" He glanced at Izzy and Celia, then up at The Dog floating near the ceiling. He frowned. "Actually, I think my dog should be first, don't you? I see he's irritated you. He's irritated me as well, by teaching you how to do magic. His intentions were not, I think, what they seemed. Dog!" he called upward. "I appreciate the fact that I'm not a rock, but your services are no longer necessary! Good-bye!"

And then The Dog pushed through the ceiling, breaking beams and showering drywall on everyone below.

"Dog!" shouted Izzy.

"Please, Peter!" said Celia.

By the time Peter had wiped the dust from his eyes, The Dog was disappearing into the night, framed by the hole in the ceiling, his small white body dwindling to nothing more than a speck rocketing toward the stars. If Peter didn't act, and act quickly, The Dog was going to die. Despite his anger, Peter instinctively thought The Dog still.

It wasn't easy to do. Peter could feel The Dog straining against the pull of his magic; Peter could slow but not stop the movement of that small furry body.

At first the magician looked confused. Then his gaze lit on Peter. "Are you...? You are! You're trying to save him!"

Peter didn't say anything. Fighting the magician's spell was hard, and the longer he tried to do it, the harder it became. He could already feel sweat beginning to bead on his forehead.

"Very interesting," said the magician. Unlike Peter, he seemed untroubled by the effort of their magical tug-of-war. "I'm not sure I understand what's going on after all. You were about to destroy him. Now you're doing everything in your power to stop him from dying. Why? What is he to you?"

Peter didn't know the answer to the magician's question. It was hard to think and do magic at the same time!

"We love The Dog," said Izzy.

The magician snorted. "Magicians don't love. Love is for ordinary people. Right, Peter?" He leaned in close to Peter's face, so close that Peter could feel his breath against his cheek. "Or maybe you're not all the way a magician yet. Maybe that's why you're having such a hard time battling my power. You're only dealing with a trickle of it, you know. That's one good thing about being a rock: I've never felt so rested in my life."

"Peter's way stronger than you," said Izzy.

The amusement left the magician's face. "Well, aren't you a sweet little peach of a girl? Only, I don't like little girls, especially sweet ones. The thing is, I have enough power to take care of you and my dog at the same time. Shall I make Peter choose between you? That might be amusing. Then you can see who the better magician is."

Panic filled Peter. High above them in the night sky, The Dog was pulling away from the earth. Peter knew, even if Izzy didn't, who the stronger magician was. To make matters worse, Peter's anger was fading by the moment as fear took its place.

"Peter will save me," said Izzy, but Peter could hear the tremor in her voice.

"I guess we'll see," the magician growled, and his eyes narrowed.

"No!" shouted Celia.

"Stop!" said Peter.

"For Izzy!" shouted a voice, more frightened than ferocious, as the closet door burst open and a skinny teenage boy threw himself through the air and onto the magician.

"Henry!" shouted Izzy, clapping her hands in delight.

"My waiter?" said the magician as he landed on his bottom on the ground, the waiter on top of him.

Peter felt it the moment the magician's spell over The Dog broke. He knew it was astonishment, nothing else, that did it: the magician had not expected the mouse-waiter's sudden attack. Just like that, the upward pull Peter had been struggling against disappeared as The Dog began to plummet back to earth. Peter thought with all the power he had left, and a second later, The Dog stood in the middle of Peter's carpet. *Oh, thank goodness,* thought Peter. *The Dog will take care of us now.* Then he realized that The Dog was blue with cold and shivering uncontrollably. He didn't look like a force to be reckoned with; he looked as if he needed to be wrapped in a blanket and held.

The magician pushed the waiter aside, then got up from the floor, shaking his head. "This has been entertaining, but I have a house to get back to. First, though, I need to dispose of the lot of you. Dust or stone? Or— I've got it...." He turned to glare at Henry, whose eyes were wide and fearful. "I don't know how you came to be here, Waiter, but you will no longer have the honor of serving me. I'm thinking you ought to be a mouse again." Henry began to shrink, pale brown fur sprouting all over his body. At the same time, he clutched at his throat. "Of course, I don't see any need for you to be able to breathe," the magician continued.

"Are you okay, Henry?" asked Izzy. "Peter, something's wrong with Henry!"

The magician laughed, a cold sound that cut through the room. "You have bigger problems than a dying mouse," he said to Peter. "In fact, you're going to be very busy. It seems I'm in need of a new waiter, and you should do perfectly. I suspect I'll be able to find jobs for your sisters as well, perhaps at my carnival."

Peter opened his mouth to argue or beg, but no words could squeeze out of his suddenly dry throat. Next to Izzy, Henry, halfway between human and mouse, had dropped to the floor, his paw-hands clawing desperately at his now bewhiskered nose.

"It will be simple enough," said the magician. "A mere matter of removing what's human about you. Your intelligence. Your soul. Your will and desire. Hold still for a minute. I've never done this before, but I'm pretty sure it's going to hurt." The magician reached out his hand, palm upward, his narrow fingers grasping at something only he could see.

Anger, Peter thought. *I have to get angry, and I'll be able to do magic.* But all he could feel was fear.

And then all he felt was pain. It was as if the magician had reached through Peter's rib cage and encircled Peter's heart with his fist. Squeezing, the magician tugged, and tugged again, more insistently; *one more tug,* Peter thought, *and my heart will slide out, and nothing will ever put it back again.*

"Stop!" cried Izzy, tears streaking down her face. "You have to stop!" But the magician didn't. As Peter watched, Celia launched herself toward him, but before she was halfway across the room, the magician waved his hand and she froze in her tracks. *Somebody help me!* Peter wanted to scream. But poor Henry was now more mouse than boy, a small brown blob writhing on the ground; and though The Dog's teeth were bared, Peter knew he could do nothing against magic as powerful as the magician's. No one could save Peter: they needed Peter to save them.

The pressure from the tugging grew and grew and grew, until the pain of it was the only thing left in the world.

And then he heard something.

It was soft at first, and he could hardly make it out. *Music,* he thought as it got louder, and then: *Not just music, a woman singing a lullaby.* The voice was unfamiliar, and the song was one Peter had never heard. He couldn't tell where it was coming from.

"In a house on a street,"

the voice sang,

"In a city that's sleeping,
A baby woke up, and
A mother rocked her son."

The song might have been unknown to Peter, but its effect was immediate: the tugging within him became less.

"And he cried, and she kissed him
And the city slept around them.
And she laughed, and he smiled,
And she sang him this song."

The song ended, but the woman's gentle voice didn't stop. "Time to sleep now, Daniel," she said. "I love you, sweetheart."

The tugging, for a moment, ceased altogether.

In front of Peter, the magician's face was a mask of longing and confusion. His dark eyes were wet, and he looked almost unrecognizable to Peter, as if—for at least a moment—he had become someone else. "Now," Peter heard The Dog say, even though he was across the room and his mouth wasn't moving.

Suddenly Peter understood where the music had come from and what he was supposed to do. But how could he do magic when he wasn't angry? And how could he be angry, looking at the sad face of the boy who suddenly was not the magician? *Daniel,* the woman's voice had said. *His mother,* Peter thought.

Trying to pull power into himself, Peter thought back once more to what The Dog had said about his father, the words that had made Peter so angry that he had made the magician human. *Magic could bring him back. But it couldn't change who he is....* This time, though, when Peter imagined his father's face, it wasn't anger he felt. In his mind's eye, he could see his father smiling at him: from across a chessboard; in the kitchen as he made pancakes; with Izzy on his lap on the sofa. His father, who loved to fly planes. Who had been a part of the air force since before Peter was born. But who also loved Peter and his sisters. Who emailed every day, even when Peter didn't write back. Who had awakened Peter on that last morning because he wanted time alone with him before he left.

Peter could feel the magic building, could feel it on the surface of his skin. It was there, waiting: the magic he needed to save himself and his sisters. But how could he give power to his anger when he felt only love?

As he watched, the magician's shoulders started to straighten. "Now!" The Dog exclaimed from across the room. "Peter! Do it now!"

"Peter!" screamed Izzy. Even Celia's frozen eyes seemed to beg him to act.

The power was present; Peter's hands were trembling with it. But he wasn't angry.

The magician lifted his face.

Peter thought.

Chapter Eighteen

It didn't feel the same. The spot on his head was slightly farther up than before, and the taste in his mouth was different, sweeter somehow, more like fruit than chocolate. But still, Peter knew it was working; there was no mistaking the feeling of magic traveling through him.

Be rock.

Peter could see the moment the magician realized what was happening. His face twisted into a snarl, and the pain in Peter's chest suddenly returned, more agonizing than before. That pain almost caused Peter's magic to slip. But the look of hope on The Dog's face helped Peter focus. *Rock. Be rock.*

The magic was like nothing Peter had done before: the magician had willpower, and from the moment he felt the first tremors of the spell, he fought against it. But Peter concentrated as he had never before concentrated in his life, all his will and determination channeled toward that one crucial act of magic.

And just like that, the magician disappeared, replaced by a rock the size of a chicken.

Peter sank to the ground with relief as the pain in his chest abruptly vanished. But he didn't even have time to figure out what had happened before The Dog was standing next to him. "Not yet," barked The Dog. "You can't stop yet."

"What do I have to do now?" said Peter, his voice shaking with exhaustion. He realized the answer even as he asked the question. Her face streaked with tears, Izzy held her hands out toward her brother; in them was the small, limp body. Was it too late? Peter wondered. He might be a magician, but he was pretty sure he couldn't bring back the dead. Even a mouse.

Izzy placed Henry in Peter's open fingers.

Izzy loved the mouse, and Peter loved Izzy. He had to try. Peter thought his way into that tiny body, the magic as strange and free of anger as it had been before. At first he was certain Henry was gone, but then he felt the flicker of a heartbeat. *Maybe,* he thought, and with his mind, he pushed air into Henry's minuscule lungs. *Again. Again.* And the heartbeat grew, and the mouse came to life in his hands.

"Henry!" cried Izzy. She took the mouse from Peter and cradled him against her cheek.

"Impressive," said The Dog. "Can you unfreeze Celia?" He glanced at Peter, slumped on the floor. "Actually, let me try." A moment later, Celia stretched her arms toward the ceiling.

She looked at Henry, now crouched on Izzy's shoulder, then down at the rock. "Wow. You did it, Peter. Everything's fixed!"

Peter didn't say anything. Neither did The Dog.

"What?" demanded Celia. "Why aren't we celebrating? Peter turned the evil magician back into a rock, Henry's okay, The Dog isn't shooting through the galaxy somewhere. Why isn't everyone happier?"

Celia's right, of course, Peter thought. He glanced down at the rock. The magician would have eagerly destroyed them all. It was a good thing he was a rock again. Wasn't it? But it didn't feel like a good thing. Inside that rock was a boy whose mother had sung him lullabies, a boy who had lived in a white house with roses in the yard.

A boy whom The Dog loved. A boy whom The Dog had manipulated today with the sound of his mother's voice. The Dog knew Daniel perfectly, Peter thought— knew him so well that he had predicted how he would react to that song.

"Can I ask you something?" Peter said to The Dog.

"Yes."

Peter chose his next words carefully. "When the magician heard that coyote howling and turned himself into a rock, that wasn't an accident, was it?"

The Dog abruptly turned toward Peter. Then his legs buckled and he sank to the floor. "How did you know?"

Peter didn't answer.

The Dog stared at the carpet as though he couldn't bear to look Peter in the eye. "I couldn't do anything to stop him," he said. "He was becoming worse and worse. And one day I decided it had gone far enough. All I did was make that sound, a coyote howling, when he was deep asleep. Of course his spell couldn't work; there wasn't a real coyote there for it to work on."

"Then why did you bring me into it? Why did you to try to convince me to make him human again?" Peter asked. "I'm probably going to end up evil, and then turn into a rock myself. And it's all for nothing. So that you could make the magician human after you made him turn himself into a rock!" For a moment, Peter felt anger building within him. But then tears suddenly stung his eyes, and the anger was gone. "I thought...I thought you were my friend."

"It was the magic water bowl," said The Dog slowly. "That's no excuse, of course. After the magician turned into the rock, I knew I'd done the right thing, but I still felt horrible. He was my best friend, after all. So one day I asked my magic water bowl what it would take to make him himself again—not himself the magician, but himself the boy. And the answer I got was you."

"Because Peter's stronger than the magician," said Izzy.

"You keep saying that," said Peter, "but I'm really not. You just think that because you're my little sister."

Izzy looked at Peter as if he were being particularly slow. "You turned the magician into a rock, didn't you?"

"Well, yes, but that was just luck."

"How did you do that, Peter?" asked The Dog. "I've been wondering. I was sure we were all goners."

Peter thought back to that moment. "I don't know, honestly. I was going to ask you. I couldn't make myself angry, but the magic worked anyway."

"What?"

"I tried to make myself angry by thinking about my dad, but it didn't work." Peter shifted his weight from one foot to the other. It felt a little embarrassing to say it aloud, but he remembered clearly what he'd felt at that moment. "I was thinking about my dad. About how much... well, how much I love him."

"You did magic through love?"

Had he? Peter thought back to the way the power had flowed through him. "I guess I did."

The Dog's mouth hung open, exposing his incisors and long pink tongue. "Peter, don't you see what you're saying?" he asked. "How do you feel now? Are you angry?"

"I...I feel fine," said Peter. How could he not have noticed before? "Not angry at all."

The Dog dropped to his haunches, lifted his nose, and howled to the stars that twinkled through the ceiling.

"What are you howling about?" Peter asked. "Are you upset?"

The Dog looked at him, and there were tears in his eyes. *A dog crying,* Peter thought. *Not the strangest part of this day, but strange enough.*

"Not upset," said The Dog. "I'm howling because I'm happy. You wouldn't understand. It's a dog thing."

"Did you know people could do magic through love? Why didn't you tell me?"

"I didn't know," said The Dog. "Or I would've told you. But I sometimes wondered if maybe you would be able to find a different way to do things than he had. That's why I didn't tell you that you had to be angry that night at the golf course. It's also why I made you hear Izzy's voice when you were flying, and why I brought your sisters to the magician's house. You care a lot about your family, and I thought that might keep the anger from taking you over. But I didn't know it was the key to everything."

"Does that mean Peter won't become evil like the magician?" Celia asked. She and Izzy were listening as intently as Peter.

"I don't think he will," said The Dog. "He's not angry now, and he just did an enormous amount of magic."

He wouldn't become evil. Peter looked down at his dusty hands; he had never before felt so grateful just to be himself. "Will I still turn into a rock? I mean, will a spell backfire on me eventually, like it did with your magician?"

"That I don't know," said The Dog. "It seems possible. But then, in legends there are often good magicians, aren't there? Like Merlin, for instance—he lived to be an old man. Perhaps there's some basis of truth in those stories."

"Are you trying to say you think I could become like Merlin?" The idea struck Peter as preposterous.

But The Dog seemed to take the question seriously. "It seems more likely to me that you'll end up like him than that you'll end up a rock."

"Yay!" Izzy cheered. Celia smiled, too, but she had a calculating gleam in her eyes: Peter could tell she was already assessing how they could put his magic to use. Aside from the relief that he might not end up a rock, Peter himself felt mostly a profound disquiet. To be a magician like Merlin? Nothing about that seemed right.

He didn't want to think about it, so he looked down at the rock again instead. "None of this changes the fact that the magician is more powerful than I am. I could barely turn him into a rock. If I tried to make him into the boy he used to be, he might end up human, but still evil."

"So we just need you to be more powerful," said The Dog.

" 'Just'?"

"I don't understand," Celia interrupted. "Why do we want to figure out how to change the magician back? He wanted to steal our souls, and he tried to kill Henry. Why should we risk ourselves trying to help him?"

"He wasn't always evil," said The Dog. "He used to be a wonderful kid. That's the person I want back."

"That's what you keep saying," said Celia, her chin jutting out. "But he must've been at least a little bit evil before, or he would've learned to do magic through love, like Peter. He's a rock, and he's not going to hurt anyone else. Let's leave him like that."

"If that's what you want," said The Dog. But he looked at Peter as he said it.

"No!" Peter said in a loud voice, surprising himself.

"But why, Peter?" Celia asked.

"Because..." Peter tried to think of the answer to this question. "Because he's not perfect. But people aren't perfect. They're just...they're people." He looked at The Dog, and he could tell that The Dog understood what he was saying, even though Peter wasn't getting the words right. "It doesn't mean he deserves to be a rock."

"He used to throw the Frisbee for me for hours," said The Dog. "I would watch for him when he came home from school. He would walk in the door and give me a treat, before he did anything else. At night I slept at the foot of his bed, and he didn't care if I snored."

"We have to change him back," said Peter. The depth of his certainty surprised him. "And we have to do it tonight."

"I wish you could use his power," said Izzy, "the way you did when you were touching the rock."

"I don't think that will work," said Peter. "He's too strong for me to control."

The Dog's ears suddenly perked up. "But I think I know whose power you can use."

Chapter Nineteen

"Absolutely not," said Peter flatly, looking at Celia and Izzy. "It would be dangerous. You could get hurt."

The Dog's idea, once he explained it, was simple enough, and Celia and Izzy wanted to help. But Peter was not going to put his sisters at risk. Not again.

"Remember when Henry jumped on the magician?" Izzy asked Peter. "He didn't have to. But he did, even though he's scared of magic and loud noises and especially the magician. It was because he knew it was the right thing to do, wasn't it, Henry?"

On Izzy's shoulder, Henry bobbed his tiny brown head up and down. Now that he was really a mouse again, he seemed a lot less, well, mouse-ish. He hadn't run for a dark closet yet, and unlike before, he seemed perfectly willing to answer questions.

"Helping the magician is the right thing to do," said Izzy. "And Celia and I want to do it."

"Besides that, you're not the boss, Peter," Celia added. "You may be the oldest, and the magician, but I've been telling you all along that you can't do everything alone. You need us, and you know it."

She was right, Peter thought. He did need them, and they were in their own ways as much a part of this as he was. Reluctantly, he nodded at The Dog.

In preparation, The Dog wished the picture of the magician from the magician's house, then handed it to Peter, Celia, and Izzy to study. "The physical details aren't important," warned The Dog. "You've seen him already. What I want you to remember is how happy he looks. He hasn't smiled like that in almost a year."

Peter stared down at the boy's face, trying to memorize the ways in which it was different from the magician's. *His grin,* he thought. *The light in his eyes. The mischievous way he looked at the camera.* After a moment or two, Celia and Izzy said they were ready, and Peter put the picture aside. Without speaking, the three children and The Dog formed a circle, holding hands and paws, with the rock in the middle.

Peter took a deep breath. The last two times he'd fought with the magician, he'd barely survived. But this time, he told himself, he wouldn't be alone. Everyone had magic, The Dog had reminded the children; it was just that most people's brains weren't capable of using it. But just as Peter had used the magician's magic when he was touching the rock, The Dog believed that perhaps Peter could borrow his sisters' and The Dog's magic for a little while. If they all thought the same thing, Peter's power might be greater than the magician's.

Peter checked once more the back corners of his mind: Angry Peter truly was gone. He was, he thought, the luckiest boy who had ever lived. He let that feeling of luck and love fill him.

The Dog had insisted that the four of them stand exactly so, but it wasn't until the magic started gathering in Peter's head that he understood why. From the first time he had done magic, Peter had sensed that power vibrated over objects and in and out of people. What he didn't realize was that even when he was thinking magic, that power was still traveling through him, only a portion of it stopping in his brain long enough for him to use it. But in the circle he, his sisters, and The Dog had formed, magic came in but didn't go out; the circle trapped it, whipping it around and around like water in a whirlpool. Peter let the swirling power build as long as he could bear it, until his hands were shaking against his sisters'.

Then he looked down at the rock. No, it wasn't a rock, he reminded himself. It was Daniel, a boy.

Daniel, Daniel, Daniel, he thought.

The rock stayed a rock for longer than seemed possible, even as Peter focused all his power on it. Then, shaking, it began to stretch, growing bigger and bigger until it was taller than Peter. But it was still a rock. *Daniel,* Peter thought, but he couldn't make the boy appear, no matter how hard he concentrated.

His vision blurring, Peter blinked. When his eyes reopened, the rock had become the magician, snarling with anger. Peter's stomach clenched in fear, and the magician could tell: grinning, he raised his arm, just as he had when he had tried to remove Peter's will. Peter's magic wavered. Celia squeezed his hand, though hers was trembling, too. On the other side, Izzy's fingers were firm and warm in Peter's own.

And Peter refocused his mind and thought back once more to the laughter in the eyes of the boy in the photograph. "You aren't real," he said to the furious magician whose face was so close to his own. "Daniel is real."

Just like that, the magician was gone. Though the boy who replaced him looked the same, he wasn't; he was someone else entirely.

Peter let go of his sisters' hands.

Bewildered, Daniel stared around the room. At first, he seemed confused, as if he didn't know where he was or what had happened. Then he began to remember. Peter could see it on his face—the way his eyes grew wide and fearful, his lips parted, and tears began to slide down his cheeks.

"I didn't mean to!" he wailed. "I'm so sorry. So sorry about everything!"

It was awful to watch. Peter opened his mouth, hoping to say something that might comfort the crying boy, but he couldn't think of any words. Izzy's hands flew to her lips, and even Celia looked horrified by Daniel's pain.

Without saying a word, The Dog trotted to Daniel's side, then butted his head against Daniel's legs. "Oh," said Daniel, and he dropped to his knees on the rug, burying his face in The Dog's fur.

And then Daniel was gone.

"Where did he go?" asked Peter.

Alone in the middle of the floor, The Dog sighed. "I sent him home."

"He was so sad," said Izzy. "Will he be all right?"

"I think so," said The Dog. "I took his memory away. I felt bad doing it, but it seemed like the only choice. In just a moment, he's going to walk into his parents' bedroom, and they'll be overjoyed to see him. And neither he nor they will ever be able to figure out where he's been these past months. It's not perfect, but it's the best we can do."

In all Peter's planning to change the magician back to his former self, he had never thought to wonder what would happen to him after that. Now he imagined what it must be like for the magician, standing by his parents' bed and not remembering any of the terrible things he'd done. Not remembering the power he'd had, the way the magic had tasted on his tongue, the way it had felt to wish and know that what you wanted would come true...

"Magic can do that?" Peter asked. "I thought you said magic couldn't change who someone was."

The Dog swiveled his ears reflectively. "Magic won't change who a person is fundamentally. But forgetting: that's a relatively minor thing. Just a shift in the surface, not a rebuilding of someone's core."

For a moment, they all stood there, staring at the spot on the floor where the rock had been. "So we did it," said Izzy. "We saved the magician, just like The Dog wanted!" She patted The Dog's head; he thumped his tail.

"What's next?" asked Celia.

The Dog looked around. "I guess the next thing is to clean up this room. And then go to bed. See what tomorrow brings."

Celia grinned. "We're going to have some awesome adventures, aren't we?"

"I want to be a bird again!" said Izzy. "Peter, can we do that tomorrow?"

"No," said Celia. "The first thing we ought to do is visit Dad. If Peter can't bring him here, we could go there, couldn't we? There must be some way. Maybe The Dog could turn into a dragon again and we could ride on his back."

"Could we do that, Dog?" said Izzy. "It sounds like fun!"

The Dog cocked his head. "It's a long way. Too long to fly, I think, even for a dragon. But maybe—"

"No," said Peter.

Three sets of eyes turned to stare at him. "What do you mean, no?" asked Celia.

"I mean, I don't want to do any more magic. Not for anything."

"But, Peter," said Izzy, "I know I made you promise, but that was when magic was making you horrible."

"Think of how much fun we could have," said Celia.

"No," said Peter again, his voice weaker this time. He couldn't think how to explain what he felt to his sisters. All he knew was that this planning, this daydreaming, felt utterly wrong to him.

"But, Peter—" said Celia.

The Dog interrupted. "Peter, can you tell us what it is you want?"

There it was, the same question The Dog had asked him on the golf course. "I want..." For a moment, Peter got stuck, trying to put words to what he felt. The Dog thought he might end up like Merlin, but that wasn't what Peter wanted. He closed his eyes and what he saw was himself, sitting at the kitchen table with his mother and sisters, arguing about dinosaurs and green beans. "I want to be myself again. The kid who didn't know how to do magic."

"Like the magician," said The Dog.

"Yes," said Peter, finally recognizing the emotion he'd been feeling when he thought about the magician. It was envy. "Like the magician."

Celia stared at Peter as though he had gone crazy. Izzy, on the other hand, turned to The Dog. "Can you do that?" she asked.

The Dog looked thoughtful. "It would be more complicated than it was for the magician. It wouldn't make sense for all three of you—and your mother!—to forget the last three days entirely. But it seems possible that we could alter your memories to make it as if this had never happened. If that's really what you want, Peter."

At The Dog's words, Peter hesitated. Did he really want to make it as though this had never happened? He thought again about the kid at the dinner table three days earlier: how powerless that boy had felt. How angry he had been. He was, Peter realized, a different person now, and he liked the ways in which he had changed. Still, he didn't want to be a magician. He knew it as surely as he knew his own name. "Okay," he said resolutely.

Izzy's hand flew to her shoulder, where Henry lay nestled in her hair. "Does everything have to go back to the way it was? Every single thing?"

The Dog gave a quiet snort of doggy laughter. "Maybe we can find a way for someone to keep her pet mouse, if that's what she wants."

"Yes, please," said Izzy.

Celia opened her mouth as if she might object. Peter braced himself for a storm of recriminations. But Celia surprised him. "Are you sure?"

"I'm sure," said Peter.

"We won't get to see Dad." It was a statement, not a question.

"I know."

Celia studied him a moment longer. Then she sighed. "All right, then. Let's get it over with."

Chapter Twenty

It took a little planning. But within what seemed to Peter to be a remarkably short time, they were ready. Holding hands again, Peter, Celia, Izzy, and The Dog began putting things right.

There was a lot to undo. First the plants that had been servants, which Peter left sitting in pots on a nearby nursery's doorstep, and the fossils, which he sent deep underground, wishing them back where they belonged. Then the magician's house, which Peter happily crumbled to dust. Some details were practical, like cleaning up the mess in Peter's bedroom. Others were less so: *Be happy,* Peter thought into the dreaming minds of the magician's old neighbors, the ones whose lives he had messed up. Peter didn't know if this would work, but it seemed worth trying.

When it was all done, Peter turned to his sisters, whose hands were still clasped in his.

"This is really okay with you?" he asked. To choose to lose his own memories was one thing: to force his sisters to lose theirs was something else.

"It's okay," Izzy said. "As long as Henry gets to stay."

Celia pressed her lips together. "Go ahead."

Forget, Peter thought, staring at their faces. *Forget the mushroom in the box, forget the room full of dinosaurs, forget driving through the night in a little yellow car. Forget the magician. Forget magic.* Izzy's and Celia's suddenly confused expressions told Peter that the magic had worked. *Bed,* he thought, and they were gone.

"I guess that's it," he said.

The Dog snorted. "Well, almost. You still have to do something about me."

"Umm. Yes." This was the one thing they hadn't talked about, any of them. Peter cleared his throat. "I'm assuming...I mean, you didn't say...but you'll need to tell me how to send you back. To your old master, I mean. Do you want me to take away your memories, too?"

"I could go back," said The Dog. There was a long pause. "But it might be logical to consider other possibilities, too."

"Other possibilities? Like what?"

The Dog pawed at the carpet. "Well, for instance, I could stay here. With you."

Peter felt a tightness in his chest suddenly loosen. "Really? You'd want to stay with me? What about Daniel?"

"I wanted to help Daniel," The Dog said. "And I'm really glad he'll be okay. But I'd like to stay with you. I mean, if you'll have me."

"I'd like it if you stayed," said Peter.

The Dog's tail curled. "Good. Then that's settled."

"But..."

"But what?"

"You won't mind if you have to go back to being an ordinary dog? Because if I'm going to go back to being the boy I used to be, I can't have a talking dog. It wouldn't make any sense."

"I know," said The Dog. "I think it will be a relief to just be a dog again, actually. Dog biscuits and fetch: it's not a bad life, after all. I do get a little tired of kibble, but if every now and then you slipped me a bite of steak and onions, well..." He tilted his nose thoughtfully. "But you do know, Peter, you'll never be exactly the same as you were? You can forget what happened. But you won't be the same."

"I wondered," said Peter. "Do you think I'm making a mistake?"

"I think the reason you're so powerful," The Dog said, "is that you don't really want to be a magician. You want to be you. That's the reason you're capable of great things—but I don't think you need magic to do them."

"Thank you," said Peter. "For everything you've done."

"You've got it wrong," said The Dog. "I should be the one thanking you." He settled his haunches on the carpet. "Well?"

"Well, what?"

"What are you waiting for? Make me ordinary, already."

Peter stared down at The Dog's face. The long, warty nose, the sharp, pointed ears. The dark dog eyes. He remembered how those eyes had scared him the first time he and The Dog had sat here: it was only three days ago, but it seemed like a lifetime. What would The Dog be like if he weren't, well, The Dog? No point in worrying about it, Peter told himself; soon Peter wouldn't remember that he'd ever been different.

And with that, Peter concentrated on the spot two inches behind his right temple and thought the magic out of The Dog.

When he was finished, he looked down. The Dog was still sitting on the floor, in the exact spot he'd been in a moment earlier. "Dog?" Peter said softly.

The Dog thumped his tail but otherwise didn't respond.

Peter reached down to scratch between The Dog's ears. He hadn't, he realized, ever done that before. The fur was rougher than he expected, but it felt good against his fingertips, and for several minutes he kept scratching. Eventually, The Dog's eyes closed, and he fell asleep, his growling snores echoing through Peter's bedroom.

And then Peter was alone.

The Dog had told him what to do; now it was up to Peter to do it. He settled back in his bed and pulled his covers up. *Think,* he told himself. But something felt wrong, and he didn't do the magic. Instead he lay there a moment, staring at his ceiling, the hole in it repaired, now back to what it had always been: water-stained and imperfect. It was once again itself, just as Peter soon would be himself. Which was what he wanted. Right?

And then Peter knew what he had to do.

He slipped out of bed and walked to his desk, stepping lightly past the sleeping dog. He powered on his computer, then watched his emails download. His father's morning email hadn't yet arrived, he saw: it was too early. That didn't matter. Peter hit the New Mail button, then started typing.

Hi, Dad,

I've been thinking about you a lot lately. I miss you. Izzy and Celia and Mom do, too. It isn't the same here without you. Nothing ever feels all the way right, you know? I bet you miss us, too. Sometimes I wonder why you left. I know you've always been in the air force. But you love us, right? So why did you go? Maybe you don't have an answer. But if you do, will you tell me? Because it's something I think about all the time, and sometimes it makes me angry. And it might make me feel better if I understood.

I hope you had a good day. I'll try harder to write you real letters from now on.

Love,

Peter

There. It wouldn't matter if he woke up tomorrow to find out he was once more the boy he had been three days ago; he still would've written this. He moved to hit the Send button but didn't; instead, he let the cursor hover there, above it. He didn't know exactly who he would be tomorrow, but whoever he was, it seemed right to let that kid decide whether he had the courage to tell his father how he felt. Hoping the answer would be yes, Peter pictured his father's face. *Be safe,* he thought.

Leaving the file open on his desktop, he went back to his bed. He slid between his sheets and lay back on his pillow. Then he thought away his memories of the last three days.

Epilogue

I wake up in the middle of the night: the floor is cold and hard, and for a moment I can't quite think where I am. Then I see Peter in the bed, and the last few days come back in a rush.

Dogs don't smile. I know that better than anyone. But for the first time in years, I've woken up happy.

I lick my tail and wonder when I'm going to tell Peter that the spell he did on me may not have worked the way he intended. Maybe I'll give it a week or two, or a month, even. The kid's had a crazy few days. But eventually I'll tell him. I'm thinking his heart wasn't in it—you've got to really want something when you do magic. Or maybe it's just that some people, no matter how much they think they ought to be ordinary, are meant for something more. And Peter, well, he was meant for me.

And I don't do boring.

I jump up next to him and curl into a ball, pressing myself against his side. Tomorrow's a new start, isn't it? Might as well begin by making it clear that I get a spot on the bed. I go to sleep trying to imagine what name Peter will give me. It better not be Darling.